In my Dreams

ELIN ANNALISE

In My Dreams

Elin Annalise asserts the moral right to be identified as the author of this work.

First published in August 2020
This edition published in April 2021 by Ineja Press

Cover Design by Elin Annalise and Sarah Anderson
Interior Formatting by Sarah Anderson

Paperback ISBN: 978-1-912369-28-7
eBook ISBN: 978-1-912369-27-0

The author can be contacted via email at ElinAnnalise@outlook.com

Second Edition, April 2021

ELIN ANNALISE

In my Dreams

INEJA PRESS

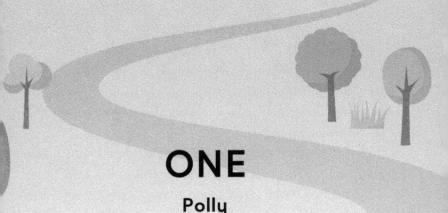

ONE
Polly

"WAIT, YOU'RE GOING on holiday with complete strangers?" Brooke stares at me from her bed across our room.

She's stretched out on her stomach, laptop on her pillow, and the sound of the latest news report blares from its speakers: *"Four men believed to have been involved in this series of attacks across the region are thought to be hiding in the south-west of the country. Police have advised…"*

"Yeah," I say, adding another pair of socks to the suitcase on my bed. "That's the whole point of it."

"A dating *holiday*?" Brooke speaks loudly, as if checking she's heard me correctly. She turns down the volume on her laptop—which is how I know she's serious about this. She absolutely loves listening to the news and usually nothing will make her turn down the volume. "With absolute strangers?"

I roll my eyes and glance out the window. The rolling moorland hills of Goldwater Nature Reserve surround us on all sides. "We're all on the asexual spectrum. I told you about it before."

"You did—but you didn't mention that you don't actually know these people." She sits up and swings her legs over the side of the bed. "You can't go on holiday with strangers. Polly, that's too dangerous."

"But that's the point—so we meet new people. I mean, I haven't exactly had much luck finding aces in the wild."

Normally, Brooke would laugh at that—we always try to say *in the wild* as much as possible. I'm not sure how exactly it started, but it's been an in-joke with us for years. But she doesn't laugh. She just rubs the hollow at the base of her neck where the tattooed birds are. It was the very first tattoo she got. "Polly, they could be anyone. They could be axe-wielding murderers or *anyone*."

"It's with a company," I say. "It's perfectly fine. They did background checks on all of us." Well, I don't know that that's entirely true, but we all had to upload photo ID and bank statements to prove our identities when we signed up. "And it's not like I'll be on my own with *one* person who could be a creep or whatever. It's a group retreat. We're all staying in the same cottage. Perfectly safe." I give her what I'm sure is a very reassuring smile.

"A cottage? As in tiny rooms where you'll be living on top of each other?" Brooke shakes her head. Her dark hair tumbles over her shoulders, rich and glossy. "All horror films start with people gathering in a cottage." Horror films are Brooke's other love. I suppose both horror films and the news often focus around crime and disaster.

From the floor below—where three more bedrooms for live-in staff are located—there's a loud clanging sound. Sounds travel easily around here. The block's pretty basic, paper-thin walls. And the floors too. Lisa's always moaning if Brooke or I walk in our room in shoes. Says it sounds like elephants stampeding above her room.

"It's fine, okay? Look, it's all paid for. I've got to finish packing." I give her a smile.

Brooke doesn't look convinced, but I return to sorting out all my clothes. I haven't got many nice ones—mostly, I wear jeans and a jacket with the Goldwater Nature Reserve's logo on it. It's a silhouette of a bird, enclosed in a circle, with the text wrapping around the circle. I quite like the logo but Lisa's thinking of updating it and asked Brooke for her artistic opinion on it.

Brooke and I both live and work here. I'm a ranger, and she's in the research team, studying cormorants at the moment. Something about their flight patterns. The two of us have been best friends since we were little. And we tell each other everything—except I didn't mention this holiday earlier, because I knew how she'd react. Even if *she* is always going out on dates. But because I'm asexual, she's strangely protective of me. Like she thinks men are going to try to hurt me or pretend to be ace in order to prove they can 'convert' me. I mean, that did nearly happen once, so I get where Brooke's coming from. I just wish she wasn't so protective.

"Well, give me the address and number of where you're staying," Brooke says as I place my one and only dress into my suitcase. It's not even a particularly fancy thing. It's brown and knee-length. Made from cotton. I mean, it sounds horrible when I put it like that. Brooke's pointed out many a time that I should get some nicer dresses. "And you better call me every evening."

"Of course," I say, pushing my hair back away from my face. My hair-tie snapped earlier, and I look around for a moment until I spot a spare on my desk. It's next to the Buddha that I got a couple years ago when Brooke and I were shopping. The majority of Brooke's family are Buddhists, and when my parents and brother were killed, I suddenly found myself spending a lot of time with the Kaos, and I discovered the teachings of the Buddha to be very helpful and calming. Grounding.

"And I'll be back in no time. Possibly after a little summer romance." I give my brightest smile, even though I am nervous. Of course I am. Brooke's right. These *are* strangers. I don't even know how many people will be there, beside the organizers.

But that's part of the fun of it. And I love things that get my heart pounding. It's why I love psychological thrillers, both books and movies.

Brooke nods. Outside in the hall, we hear the Grandfather clock chiming. Six o'clock. The canteen will be open now for dinner. I shove a few more clothes in the suitcase. Think that will be enough. It's only for two weeks, and there's a washing machine at the place.

"You coming?" I ask Brooke.

She nods, and we grab our handbags, slip shoes on by the door, and then shut the door behind us and check the handle. It usually locks automatically, but a couple times it hasn't. Of course, nothing was stolen; this block only houses the live-in rangers and research staff and we all trust each other, well…mostly.

I make light conversation with Brooke as we head down toward the canteen. The other staff—both live-in and day-timers—appear and by the time Brooke and I reach the large, open room of the canteen and are loading our plates up with spaghetti bolognaise and vegetables, there's a strong buzz about the place. I like this buzz. Like feeling like part of a community. Having a *family*. People who care about me.

After my parents and brother died in a car accident, three years ago, I never thought I'd find this sense of belonging again. But Goldwater's been great to me. They are my family now.

Brooke and I sit down at our usual table, opposite each other, and—

"Oh my God," she whispers, her eyes fixed on something behind me.

"What?" I turn and—

And everything stops.

Sitting four tables away is Harry Weller.

Harry Weller.

Electricity runs through me.

I am dreaming. I have to be dreaming. This can't be real. The man I've always been in love with cannot be sitting a mere twenty feet from me. He just can't.

My heart races, and adrenaline pumps through me. It's *him*. Dark eyes, long blond hair, creamy skin, a sharp jawline, a muscular build. Harry Weller, looking like a Viking. He's filled out even more in the years since I've seen him. Filled out very well....

"What's he doing here?"

I jump and turn back to Brooke. She's holding her fork halfway to her mouth, spaghetti and sauce trailing from it, but has made no move to eat it.

I hastily swallow the spaghetti in my mouth. "I don't know…" I flick another glance in his direction, then tell myself to calm down.

But Harry Weller is here. I haven't seen him since we were eighteen—him and me and Brooke were all at the same sixth form. I was completely in love with him. And now seven whole years have passed, and just the mere sight of him has all those feelings flooding back.

I look back at Brooke, quickly. The rings on her fingers catch the light and dazzle me for a second. Brooke likes rings. I mean, I do too, but I only have one. My small black band that I always wear. Brooke, on the other hand, has a whole collection of them and she picks out three or four to wear each day, choosing them based on the colors of her makeup and overall style. Says the rings make her fingers look longer. And they do. Everything about her is slender and beautiful and artistic. She's like a model—but *more*. She has more *life*. Birds are tattooed all over her body, in both abstract and realistic designs, and she has the ability to make even the Goldwater uniform look like it's been made for a catwalk. I know at least two of the men in the research team are pining over her, not to mention Grant, one of the other rangers. Last time I was on duty with him, he kept trying to subtly ask me about her and whether Brooke has a boyfriend.

But Brooke doesn't really do boyfriends. She dates a lot, has sex a lot (as she's always telling me), and has fun. She's wild, a free spirit. Yet every guy who falls in love with her—and there have been many—seem to think she'll settle for him. They're always convinced of it.

Just like how I was convinced that one day at school, Harry Weller would notice me—really notice me. As more than a friend. That he'd walk up to me and we'd kiss and it'd be passionate and intimate and perfect. It's embarrassing how many times I planned out how it could happen.

Brooke frowns. "Oh no—Pols, *no*." She gets the squinty look she always does when she's concentrating. She says that came about because of too many hours peering through binoculars waiting for whichever species she was watching to do whatever it was she was waiting for.

"No?"

"You can't pine after him again. I am not reliving GCSEs and A-Levels again with that level of angst. *Oh, why doesn't he notice me, B?*"

I laugh, but it sounds false to my ears. Because of course it's false. "I'm over him," I lie. "No worries there. I mean, it's been years."

"Good," Brooke says. "Easiest for us all."

"And I'm going on a *dating* holiday tomorrow. But that doesn't stop me from wondering what he's doing here." I take a sip of my coffee. Then I wonder if I've given myself a frothy moustache and hurriedly wipe the back of my hand across my mouth—just in case Harry gets up and walks past and happens to look over here.

He doesn't. Another subtle look behind me tells me he's eating his food slowly and carefully. His phone's on the table by his tray, and he's peering intently at it. He always loved reading graphic novels, when we were at school. Maybe he's reading one now.

Or maybe he's reading a message from a girlfriend, the voice in my head says when I turn back around.

Brooke gives me another warning look.

"It's okay!" I say again, a little loudly, and the rangers at the next table look over. Grant looks concerned—but, then again, he often looks like that anyway. Especially if there's anything that could possibly indicate Brooke's upset.

My best friend doesn't look convinced, and we eat our meal with her giving me knowing glances all the time. Bet she'll be secretly glad I'm flying off tomorrow to Paris, so she doesn't have to listen to me pine over Harry.

That's if he's even staying here….

"I'm heading off now," Brooke says, getting up from the table once she's finished. She grabs her jacket and bag from the spare chair next to her. "But I'll see you for tonight's obs?"

"Yeah," I say. "You coming back to the room first?"

She nods.

"Perfect. See you there."

Brooke heads out, and I stay sitting at the table, wondering if Harry's finished his food yet and whether he's noticed me. Not that he'd recognize me from the back…would he?

No, it doesn't matter.

A screech of chair legs on the tile floor jolts my attention behind me. To Harry. He's finished his dinner and is heading out. He doesn't pause, like he's wondering which way to go. No, he looks like he knows the way. His strides are confident and purposeful. But what is he doing here? He doesn't work here. And we've had no vacancies for rangers, researchers, admin staff, or the maintenance team. Plus, it would just be weird if a person whom Brooke and I both went to school with got work here too. I mean, I'm only here because Brooke got me this job. But neither of us has got Harry a job here too. And what are the chances of it happening by coincidence?

I gather my things and head back to my room. It's strange, walking through the block when it's deserted. I've got today off, but everyone else is still working now that our dinner break is over.

I'd imagined I'd be finishing my packing during this time between dinner and helping Brooke with the observations, but that can wait. And, anyway, I can finish it super quickly later, if need be. It's not like I have a lot of amazing clothes to assess and decide which to take. Right now, I need to know why Harry Weller is here.

Once I've retrieved my laptop, I log into GolSys—the Goldwater Nature Reserve and Research Facility system. Every person in Goldwater is logged into the attendance system. Super important for fire drills and the like. And Harry was eating dinner in our canteen. The place for the staff.

He can't be working here, can he?

I scroll through the names, until I find his at the bottom.

Authorized guest.

I stare at the screen, then tap my fingers absentmindedly on the elephant stickers either side of my laptop's trackpad. And he's here for two weeks?

The two weeks when I'm going to be away.

It's like Fate knows and hates me.

Or maybe Fate doesn't hate me. Because Fate knows if I was here, I'd be being tortured by my feelings, imagining a relationship with Harry where he's asexual too—or at least willing to be with an asexual girl. A relationship where we're compatible. But if going to school with him taught me anything, it's that he's a very sexual person. And I doubt that's changed in the last seven years.

TWO
Polly

"WAIT." CLARE POINTS her plastic fork at me. "You're in love with Harry Weller?"

Heat fills my face, and I look down at the table. Damn, I could kill Brooke for telling her. But I know Brooke isn't the best at keeping secrets, and I knew that when I told her. When I finally confessed that for all these years I've been in love with Harry. I suppose it was inevitable. We grew up on the same road, played together for years as small children. He was my best friend then.

And, sure, we didn't really stay friends when my family moved away. And when we started secondary school, we were barely in any lessons together. So being in love with him when I was fourteen was fine—because he was unattainable. He was in the popular group. And I wasn't.

But now we're in sixth form, things are different. Classes are smaller and everything's more intimate. Harry and I have History and French together. I see him every day. And my heart aches more each time I see him and realize he's never seeing me in that way too.

"She is in love with him!" Rach shrieks.

"Be quiet," I hiss at her, because Harry and his friends are sitting about twenty feet away.

Most of the sixth form is outside for lunch because for once it's sunny. We're near the drama block, and we can hear the Year 7s in there practicing their end-of-year play. They must be really committed to give up their lunch for this. And when it's such great weather.

Clare frowns. "So, you're not asexual?" Her voice is low. At least she's got enough tact to know I don't want that information brandished about. Coming out to my friends was difficult enough.

"What?" I frown. "I am."

"But you're in love with Harry?"

"Being ace means I'm not interested in sex. Love is a different thing. I'm asexual, but I'm also heteromantic."

"That's a lot of labels," Rach says.

My sketchbook is open in front of me and I stare at it. The bird I'd been drawing looks pathetic—especially as I was trying to copy one of Brooke's drawings. She told me that copying would help me improve, and she gave me one of her prized notebooks that her grandparents in Taiwan gave her. Not that I'm artistic like she is. But I want to draw a picture for Mum for her birthday.

Clare snorts. "And Harry's very sexual. He slept with Annabelle and Megan at that party. You haven't got a chance with him."

My shoulders tighten. "I never said I did. And Brooke shouldn't have told you."

"Where is she, anyway? Brooke?" Rach asks. She looks worried. She knows what Clare can be like. It's not that Clare's purposefully mean— it's just her manner.

I shrug. "Probably in the common room with Brad."

I know it makes me a bad friend to admit that I'm jealous of my best friend. But ever since Brooke and Bradley got together, they've been inseparable. And it's not just that they're sleeping together, but they hang out too, they do homework together, they have Sunday lunch at each other's houses with their families. And they're so in-sync with each other.

That's what I want.

But maybe Clare's right. I can't have love without the sex. I mean, everyone in our year is so sex-mad. Always talking about it.

A shadow falls over my mangled drawing. I twist my neck and look up.

Nearly six-foot-tall, blond-haired, and with muscles only found on a rugby player.

Harry Weller.

Oh, God. He heard. He heard Clare and Rach and—

"Hey, Polly," he says, and his eyes seem to sparkle. "Are you free next period? Thought we could work on the history project."

The history project. I'd been trying not to think about how Ms. Lake partnered me with Harry. Said it was good to work with new people.

My mouth dries and my heart thumps as I look up into Harry's face. "Yeah, sure."

He grins and saunters back to his table. "See you in the common room then," he calls back.

I smile, feel awkward and uncomfortable. It was much better when Harry and I were younger and lived on the same road. When we just hung out with his sister Sara, and I wasn't in love with him. I turn back to find Clare scowling.

"He's never going to be interested in you," she says.

THREE
Polly

"OKAY, YOU READY?" Brooke looks around our room that evening.

"Ready?" I'm sprawled on my bed, finally finished with packing. I quickly put my phone down—so she can't see that I've been looking up Harry Weller on social media, trying to find out what he does now. Because it's been years. When we left sixth form, we completely lost touch. Not that we ever tried to stay in touch. It's weird how things work—as kids we were inseparable, until my parents moved to the other end of town. Then Harry and I barely spoke. Except for the history projects, and those long evenings walking around the park as we talked—it sort of became a ritual to do that once we'd finished the work.

Unfortunately, Harry's social media profiles are all set to private. Well, I suppose that's sensible.

Brooke rolls her eyes. Her radio is playing in the background—more reports on the four men at large in our county. I wish the news reports would just call them terrorists, because that's what they are. But they're white, and the racism is blatantly obvious. "Seriously? You've forgotten already? Switched shifts. Final obs tonight."

Ah yes. I blink. "Right. Yes. Five minutes. Let me get my laptop ready."

By the time we get out of the building, it's beginning to get dark. Nights still haven't started much later, even though it's mid-April. I swear Goldwater stays darker than most places.

The viewing-hut is on the eastern side of Goldwater, a fifteen-minute journey in the truck, and it smells of damp earth. I wrinkle my nostrils as we sit inside the hut. Never liked it. Brooke dumps her bag next to the mini-fridge and then hunches over a desk at the viewing platform. Her binoculars press against one of the tiny windows in the wooden boards as she watches a cormorant do its thing.

Me? I'm sitting in the research area. There's a huge cabinet system behind me where all the sightings get logged. It's not even digitized. So many scraps of paper representing years of work. And I've got to type it all up.

Well, I haven't *got to*, but I promised I'd help Brooke. She needs to compare whatever data she gets this season with previous years' results, and spreadsheets and graphs are the easiest way. Brooke switches on the radio in the cabin and tunes into a news report on the four wanted men. It's pretty much all anyone's talking about.

"Half-brothers Aleks Armstrong and Julian Fennah are believed to be in the Torbay area, while the other two men the police are still searching for, Charlie Less and Nikolai Ren, were last seen on CCTV in Barnstaple."

Hmm, we're not too far from Torbay. Goldwater's to the east of Brixam, the most southern town of Torbay. But they wouldn't actually come here, would they? Wouldn't they stick to the towns? Except it would be easier for them to be found in towns... And hiding out in nature...

I swallow hard.

"Armed police are still looking for these men, and members of the public are warned to stay vigilant, but not to approach any of these men should they see them. Instead, call the police on..."

But I'm going on holiday tomorrow. And by the time I'm back—if not later today—the terrorists will be caught.

I drone out the voices and get to work, and it's quite amazing how quickly the first hour passes.

"Are you sure this holiday's a good idea?" Brooke asks at one point.

I sigh. "Yes, it is," I say, but of course that makes me think of Harry. Because anything to do with romance does. Why is he here?

And then I feel like I'm eighteen again, just waiting for him to notice me. And possibly realize he's ace too. Which is never going to happen. I don't know why I torture myself so much.

It's a good job I'm going away.

"What time are you off tomorrow?"

"Eleven," I say.

She nods. "Well, if there are any creepy guys, leave right away. You hear me?"

It's late when Brooke and I return to the village in the four-by-four, driving it too fast over the rough ground. Brooke's driving, and she's wearing her annoyed face. She didn't get the data she wanted and we're right at the deadline now.

"Just check with Lisa," I say. "You may be able to use it."

She shakes her head. "It doesn't support the hypothesis. All this research…" She mimics the sound of an explosion. Ever-dramatic, Brooke is.

"It'll be okay," she says, then she frowns.

I look ahead and see the commotion around the village. There are two staff dorms there, with the visitor block on the far side—the block where Harry must now be staying. But there's a crowd in front of Lisa's place. And I can see Lisa, the head of Goldwater, in the middle of it. She's a small woman, but she commands presence.

Harry is in the crowd too. I notice him a heartbeat later.

"What's happening?" I frown. Everyone's milling about just after midnight. Outside? It's the fire assembly point, but I can't see any signs of a fire. No smoke in the air. Nothing.

Brooke slows the four-by-four, then parks up next to the others. We jump out.

"What's going on?" I ask.

Lisa frowns. She's the head of Goldwater, and her dark skin is weathered by all the years out in the elements. Like how farmers' faces tell you their job, how they've spent harsh winters and burning summers outside. "We all back now?" She does a quick headcount. "Okay, we're in lockdown."

"Lockdown?" several people exclaim.

"Government orders," Lisa says. "Officials believe the terrorists are in this region—they've put the whole county in lockdown. No public transport. Schools and non-essential shops are shut. We're being told to order food and essentials online until lockdown's lifted."

"So we're on holiday?" Brooke looks hopeful.

"No, we're keeping Goldwater running. Animals to look after, land to maintain, poachers to stop," Lisa says. "Could be a day we're in lockdown, could be more. Prime minister's doing regular updates."

I stare at her. "But I go away tomorrow."

"You can't," Lisa says. "We all have to stay where we are. The day-staff aren't even allowed to come in tomorrow." She looks around at all of us—me and Brooke, then the other live-in staff: Grant, Evie, Morris, Jane, and George. And Harry—because he's still here. "It can't last long like this," Lisa continues. "But, right now, we have to keep Goldwater running."

"I can help too," Harry says, his voice all rich and velvety. His words almost wrap around me. "Just show me the ropes."

My eyes fall on him. Just him, standing alone. Why is he here anyway?

"That'd be great," Lisa says. "Chances are poachers are going to take this opportunity to take more of our deer. They'll know we've got less staff, and they're not going to be bothered about breaking lockdown."

Evie's eyes widen and she looks around. "What if the terrorists are here?" she asks in the smallest of voices. Evie's a strange one—she's instantly likable because she somewhat resembles an innocent fawn. People just want to protect her and like her. But, at the same time, although I think she's nice enough, there's always been something about her that I can't put my finger on. Something that makes me a little wary.

"They won't be," Grant says. He shares the same dark eyes that his sister Lisa has, but his skin is a shade or two lighter than hers. "We've locked the gates. We're enclosed."

Except we're not enclosed. Poachers can get over the walls easy enough. What's to stop the terrorists? And what if they're already here, and we've trapped them in with us?

Evie doesn't look convinced, and I can't help but think again that a nature reserve would be an excellent place for terrorists to hide. There's no CCTV, and not enough of us staff to keep an eye on all the hundreds of acres. Not to mention, a good proportion of that is forest land. Easy to hide in there. Even if we're patrolling, chances are we won't see them.

I swallow hard.

"Now, tomorrow morning." Lisa clears her throat. "Polly, I want you out on patrol. Yes, take Harry with you, show him the ropes. All research positions are going to be put on hold. Protecting our animals is priority."

Take Harry with me? I glance toward him, then at Lisa. "Is…is he a ranger?"

"Journalist," she says. "Just show him around. We're going to need all hands on-deck."

"You're a journalist?" I turn to look at Harry. The question is out of my mouth before I can stop it, and I splutter, realize I've spoken to him. I feel myself blushing and immediately feel silly. I'm not a schoolgirl anymore. I'm a grown woman of twenty-five, so why the hell am I reacting like this?

"Yeah," he says, voice flat. "Don't look worried though. Nothing bad. Just doing a report on Goldwater to lay the grounds for next month's gala."

Ah, that gala. The big promotional effort that Lisa's been working on for months. Apparently, it's attracting a lot of rich men and women, and we're always looking for sponsors and donations.

"Okay," I say, and my voice squeaks, because *of course it does*.

I look back at Harry. Does he recognize me? I can't tell. He's not showing any signs of recognition.

But could now be my chance with him? I mean, it's not like he can avoid me here. And, he's a hell of a lot safer than some stranger on a dating holiday. Even if we are in lockdown.

And Grant and Lisa are right—the terrorists can't be in Goldwater. So we're safe here. Trapped together.

FOUR

Harry

POLLY BRADY. I'M sure it's her. I stare at her as she walks away. She's short and skinny, with very pink, somewhat sunburnt skin and mid-brown hair, and she walks with a heavy step as she follows the other woman. My breathing quickens. It's her. I'm sure it is. And the Asian woman she's following, she looks familiar too: dark hair and very pale skin, and *confidence*. So much of it. She's striking. But, still, my attention is focused on Polly. The woman showing me around here tomorrow.

It's been eight years, but I'd recognize her anywhere. The curve of her face, the sleekness of her hair, how her nose is prominent—something that she hates, but I just think it makes her face looks stronger.

And the other woman—Brooke Kao? My eyes narrow as I squint, as if by squinting I can somehow zoom in or lift the darkness and confirm my suspicions. But I'm sure it's her now. And Polly and Brooke always were inseparable at school, especially when we were seven years old.

"Hopefully this lockdown won't disrupt your work too much," Lisa says. She gestures for me to walk with her back to the block. The block where I'm staying. I'd thought it would be the visitors' block when I arrived, but Lisa told me that's mainly for school residentials. And as I'm working with the staff and my boss knows Lisa, they're housing me with the rest of their live-in staff. It's the same block Polly and Brooke are heading into.

"Of course not," I say to Lisa, giving her a grin. "Journalists are trained for all sorts of unexpected things. You think these men are nearby?" I try to keep the worry out of my voice. As I just said, we're trained for unexpected things. But it still doesn't mean that I'm not nervous.

"Impossible to know. Devon is huge," she says. Her clothes rustle as she walks. "Could be in one of the cities. Harder to find them in busy places. That's probably why they put us in lockdown. Strip the cities of the people and it's easier to find the terrorists."

Or lockdown will send the terrorists to the wilderness, I think, looking out at what I can see of Goldwater Nature Reserve. Beyond the buildings—the accommodation block, the education center, and two buildings I wasn't shown on my quick tour round Goldwater's 'village' earlier—the hills stretch out for miles, disappearing into the darkness. But there's moonlight, so I can see their shapes.

Goldwater is made up of two hundred acres of moorland, forest, and farmland. Some rare type of deer was introduced here as part of a breeding program, along with wild boar, but poachers are apparently a common problem. Antlers and tusks sell for a lot. Strange though, I'd never thought of poaching as something affecting England. I'd always thought it only applied to elephants and big animals like that. But Lisa was telling me about a guy from the British Deer Society that heads some organization fighting against poaching. Damn. Can't remember his name now. I think I wrote it down in my notebook though. That's what the gala event is for, shining the light on the poaching problems 'close to home' as my boss put it. I do worry though whether a report like this—and my boss wants me to include how much antlers and tusks sell for—will attract more poachers to Goldwater.

"You know where everything is?" Lisa asks as we step inside the accommodation block.

There's no sign of Polly or Brooke now, and something in my chest tightens.

"Yep," I reply.

"Great. Patrol begins at seven, sharp, tomorrow. You know where to meet Polly? Out by the trucks?"

I nod.

And that appears to be the end of our conversation, because Lisa enters her room and shuts the door, leaving me alone in the hallway. I take a moment to look at the décor—it's simple, but the walls are a little damp in places. Turning, I head to the staircase and make my way to my room.

Just as I'm turning the key in my door, my phone rings.

I pull it out and glance at the screen. "Mum?" I stumble over the threshold—it sticks up about half an inch, and I caught my foot on it earlier too.

"It's Sara." My sister's voice wavers, and just hearing her is a surprise. We fell out two years ago, and she never calls me now.

"What is it?" I shut my door, then sit on my bed.

Oh, God. I can feel it. Something bad has happened.

"Mum's had a fall," she says.

"What? Where is she?" I look around my room. "At hospital?"

"Yeah, Bo's taking her."

Bo's our brother. Older than both of us. In the background, I hear Mum's dogs barking. They've never been the biggest fan of my sister. Or any of us children really. Not when we were teenagers. Not now. Mum's all they have eyes for.

"Can you drive up?" Sara asks.

"To Scotland?" I feel like cursing. I knew it was a bad idea for Mum to move there. Just knew it. She's too far away from me—even if she did move there to be close to Sara and Bo, who both ended up in the north after university. But I felt betrayed by that, wanted them to stay in Devon, where we all grew up. It didn't matter that I myself had moved to London, because London's closer to Devon, and sure, I'm a hypocrite, but I hate that they've moved to Scotland. At least I'm within easy traveling distance if I need to go back. Not that we have any family there now.

I run a hand through my hair. "No, Devon's in lockdown, Sara. It was just announced—because of those attacks." I curse. "I don't know how long it's going to last. A couple days? Is it serious with Mum?"

"I don't know yet," Sara says. "Bo's gonna phone me when he knows. He's gone to the hospital with her—we don't know how long she was lying there for. Bo was just popping round and found her."

Bo visits Mum every week. He's in Glasgow, whereas my sister's two or so hours away in Newcastle.

"Thank God Bo was going then," I say.

"I'll let you know more when I know," Sara says, her voice curt.

After she hangs up, I sit on my bed, rubbing my hands together. It's a nervous habit I picked up when it was exam time in sixth form. And years later, I haven't been able to shake it. I just keep imagining all sorts of things that could happen with Mum.

Then my phone buzzes.

A text.

Bo.

Mum's okay.

I take a deep breath, a million weights lifted from my shoulders, and grab my towel. Showering always helps me unwind.

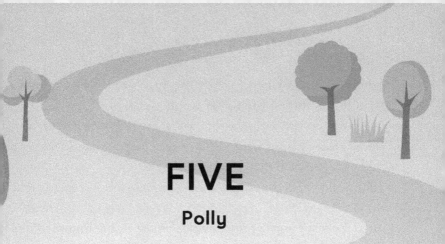

FIVE

Polly

I EMAIL THE company that runs the dating holidays for asexuals, explaining the situation and asking if I can possibly have my deposit back, but I can't stop thinking about Harry.

About how things can't possibly work between us. I mean, he's very into sex. And I'm not. And, for a lot of guys, sex is important. I know some aces have sex in order to please a partner, but I tried that once—with my boyfriend at uni. Peter knew I was ace, and we only ended up doing the act one time. He was often pressuring me—not in a forceful way. Just every now and again he'd mention 'his needs'. Or he'd call me selfish because he was making compromises being with me to suit my needs, but I wasn't making any to suit his needs. Or when we'd kiss, he'd press against me so I could feel how ready he was, even though he knew it made me very uncomfortable. And I understood that he did have needs, and he kept saying it and doing those things, and making me feel bad, so I did it in the end. Had sex. I didn't feel anything except pure revulsion. And afterward, any feelings I'd had for him had just gone. Just like that. I couldn't even stand to be in the same room as him, and it sounded stupid when I told a therapist on campus about it. About how haunted I felt after having sex with Peter.

She decided it was evidence of sexual trauma in my past (which is wrong) and wanted to counsel me for that, saying she could cure me of my 'fear of sex'.

But I didn't need a cure. I wasn't broken, but her saying that completely invalidated my identity as an asexual. Instead, I turned to a support group online for aces and found others who were sex-repulsed, like me.

I sigh. The way I liked Peter was nothing compared to my feelings for Harry. Because this is much deeper. This is like the blood flowing through my veins. My feelings for him are something that feel tangible to me, something I can reach out and hold, clench in my fist and bring close to my heart.

And it's because of that that I'm sure I can't actually do anything about Harry. I still love him deeply, and I don't want *that* to turn to resentment. I don't want to end up having sex with him and feeling haunted and having to avoid him completely as I work through the trauma that sex causes me. I need to meet someone who also gets what being ace is, who doesn't think I'm just a tease because I like kissing and physical intimacy that isn't sex.

I guess I'll just have to wait until next year to go on the dating holiday. And try not to get too close to Harry for the next two weeks. Yes, I'm going to have to avoid him.

"Best thing to do," Brooke says when I tell her my plans for avoidance after she's finished watching some documentary about crime on iPlayer, one she's been watching in ten-minute snippets whenever she has time. My plans include asking Grant to show Harry around tomorrow, instead of me.

I'd expected her to have more to say, but then again, what is there to say? She's not going to argue with me on this.

"I'm going to shower." And construct some storyline in my head, no doubt, where Harry is also ace—or at least willing to be with me and not want sex and not think that I'm a cock-tease (which I have been called before by guys in clubs, back at uni) and not be in an open relationship, because I know that just wouldn't suit me. I mean, really, I'm asking for way too much here, I'm sure. But my brain does this sort of stuff all the time, you know, constructing scenes where I find someone who loves me for who I am and they're willing to give up sex completely. And of course it only ends up torturing me because I have yet to find a guy who really gets what being ace is and respects my boundaries. And maybe it's me being selfish. I don't get why I'm so caught up on sex—and why I can't stomach the idea of just doing it with a partner or being okay with an open relationship—when I feel no sexual attraction.

I grab my towel and toiletries bag. The bathroom is just at the end of the hall.

My slippers make a scuffing sound on the soft carpet as I head toward the bathroom.

The door opens and—

Wet hair, water droplets glistening on damp skin. Abs so defined he may as well be on the cover of a magazine.

Harry.

"Oh, sorry," he says, seeing me. He steps to the side.

My mouth drops open. I may be ace, but that doesn't mean I'm not rendered speechless by the sight of him. Because I am. Especially when he's…just got a towel on. And the water droplets on his body… It's not that I'm sexually attracted to him because of the water droplets and his muscles—even though I know this is a classic scene in any romance film and I almost feel like I *should* be feeling something sexual. But, rather, it's the way the light's shining off each droplet, the healthy sculpting of his muscles, and the aesthetic of it all that makes me stare.

"I..." I say, and what the hell am I even trying to say? Who knows?

"I'm just over there." Harry points down the corridor. To the room next to mine and Brooke's.

He's staying *next door*.

How didn't I know this earlier?

Harry Weller is staying next door. To me. Right on the other side of my wall. There'll only be one wall separating us.

I feel my face flush and look away. "Uh, see you tomorrow then." I kick myself. Supposed to ask Grant to...

But what if I don't? What if I do try and see if Harry and I could work? Brooke doesn't have to know that I'm not avoiding him.

"Yeah." Harry nods. Water drips from his hair down his face, and he shakes his head in the cutest way, flicking the water away. "Polly, right?" And he looks at me with such intensity that I feel myself blushing. "You're showing me around the grounds then?"

"Yep." I nod, then I realize I've just copied what he's done by nodding. I don't think he remembers me. And I don't know whether that's a relief or not.

"Well, I very much look forward to it," he says, shaking more water droplets from his hair. He's smiling easily, and his eyes are on me. They're almost too intense. Wow, I'd forgotten how intense his gaze can be.

"Me too," I say.

His eyes drop to my towel and the toiletries bag I'm holding. "Let me get the door for you," he says, leaning back and opening it in such a way that I have to duck right under his arm.

He's still got that easy grin on his face.

My heart pounds. "Thanks." I'm sure my face must be beet-red.

Harry gives me another smile that nearly has me melting. That makes me want to be close to him. Closer than ducking under his arm would allow for... I want his skin against mine, I want that feeling of safety and intimacy with the man who was my best friend as a child and who turned out to be such a good friend to me in sixth form.

I duck under his arm, sort of gulping. The scent of his shower gel washes over me, and—

He touches my arm. Just a brush, the tiniest of touches— so light I could've imagined it.

"Nice to see you, Polly," he says. God, even his voice is beautiful. Rich and dark, like molasses.

"See you tomorrow."

Before I can fall any more in love with Harry Weller, I run into the steamy bathroom, lock the door, and turn the shower on.

When I discovered asexuality was a thing, it was a relief. I wasn't broken. I wasn't abnormal or unnatural—because up until then, I'd been told that the evolutionary purpose of humans was to breed. To have sex.

The one thing I didn't want. I just never felt any desire to have sex, never experienced sexual attraction. Wasn't interested in sex.

I wondered if I'd grow out of it. That's what a lot of forums said—not forums about asexuality. No, these were the forums I was browsing, trying to work out why I didn't 'get' sex. Why I had no interest in it when all the other girls at school were talking endlessly about boys in a very sexual way, comparing experiences and sharing gossip. And it's not that I didn't like hearing the gossip, it made me feel involved in it all and not left out, but I had no desire to lick chocolate off a naked male body or whatever it was that Clare had done recently.

I just wanted the romance. The companionship. Having someone I could be myself with. Someone to hug and cuddle all night. Even if I'd believed then that I'd have to have sex if I wanted that. A compromise.

Then I found that there were other people like me. A whole new world opened up. And it was such a relief—the validation of it was amazing.

But there aren't many aces about. And even if I do meet someone, it's not like there's immediately guaranteed to be chemistry. When I said that to Brooke once, she looked at me like I was weird. She didn't think I'd feel chemistry because she only thinks there's one type: sexual chemistry. But, for me, chemistry is emotional too. And it's about sensual attraction and feeling deeply connected. It's wanting to be around someone all the time. And it's these qualities that make me feel so connected to Harry.

It wasn't like he never knew I existed at school. I mean, we'd been best friends as kids. And though we'd grown apart, sixth form had brought us closer together again thanks to a teacher pairing us up for a project. After that first history project, we chose to work together on others. It was Harry's idea at first, and

I thought it meant he may have liked me. That he might really be *seeing* me—not as his former best friend but as an eighteen-year-old *woman*. I didn't have the killer bodies that Brooke and Clare had, but I was thinner than Rach and some of the boys in my year had rated me a seven. Yet Harry didn't seem to notice me, not in the way he did other girls. So we were just friends again. And with Brooke and Brad going out, that merged our two friendship circles even more. I went to a party once at Harry's house. And maybe it makes me sound like a stalker, I don't know, but I was always super aware of where he was. Like, I just knew.

I mull over all this as I stand under the warm water. I think this is why it really startled me suddenly seeing him in the canteen. Because I didn't know he was there, whereas at school, I instinctively knew if he was close by.

The water begins to get cold, so I turn it off and get changed quickly, before combing my hair and applying moisturizer to my face. Damn, Lisa's not going to be happy I've used all the remaining hot water.

"Your phone got a message," Brooke tells me when I return to our room. She's not smiling. "It's from Harry."

"What?" I stare at her. "He hasn't got my number."

"Facebook notification. He wants to be friends." She gives me a stern look. "What?"

"You know, when one profile is friends with another—"

"I know what being friends means." I run a hand through my wet hair. "When did he send it? He was just showering." Wait, how long was I in the bathroom?

Now, Brooke's staring at me. "You *know* he was just showering? What the hell, Polly? This isn't you keeping out of his way."

"I bumped into him on his way out the bathroom." I grab my phone from her. Sure enough. Harry Weller wants to be friends.

He must've recognized me after all. Not to mention we've got several mutual friends. If he didn't know who I was before, there's no denying he does now. The name of our school's in my profile.

Wait, does he think I deleted him before? Because we used to be friends on Facebook, when we were at school. But I deleted my profile, started again, and then couldn't bear to torture myself over seeing his photos on my feed every day. So, I never added him again.

I take a deep breath.

"You can't," Brooke says. "You can't go through this torture again. Delete the request."

"But I'm showing him round tomorrow—that's going to look rude if—"

"You said you were swapping shifts with Grant." Brooke shakes her head. "Pols, I'm saying this because I love you. But you need to swap with Grant. *Really*. Like, it's never a good idea to hang out with Harry, you know that. And in the middle of a *terrorist lockdown*?"

"I know," I say, at the same time as I click to accept the friend request.

"Deleted the friend request?" Brooke asks.

"Yes," I lie. And I hate that I'm lying to my best friend, but I've got to see if there's anything between me and Harry. I have to give us a chance.

And it's too late to undo it now anyway. I'm now friends with Harry Weller. I breathe deeply and—

My phone vibrates.

A message from him.

Brooke flicks a glance at me, doesn't say anything.

I sit on my bed, my phone out of her vision. Click on the message.

Sorry for being scantily dressed out there, Polly. I'm not usually in such a state of undress around beautiful women.

Heat rushes to my face. He thinks I'm beautiful? And he was aware of how little he was wearing?

Well, of course he was.

But he thinks I'm beautiful!

Brooke sighs. She's got her phone now and stares at her screen. "You accepted it, I can see that you're friends with him. Polly, think about it. You're just going to get hurt. I mean, romance films never have an allo guy ending up with an ace woman—and that's for a reason. You need to find someone who's like you."

Someone who's like me. As if I'm a whole different species.

"But I can't get on the dating holiday now," I say.

"So, wait another year."

I make a non-committal noise. Neither agreeing nor disagreeing.

I cross over to the window. Outside, it's dark, but under the security light I can see Moggie, the resident domestic cat at Goldwater. And she is one fat cat. Practically like a ginger sphere on legs. Morris overfeeds her, that's for sure.

But I can't concentrate on Moggie now. Because Harry Weller thinks I'm beautiful. And tomorrow, I'm spending the day with him. He's got to have messaged for a reason. And maybe, just maybe, he knows I'm asexual and is okay with it.

I feel the excitement rise within me. I can't let this opportunity pass. I need to know one way or another. And I'd been looking forward to romance over the next two weeks—even if I'd been doubtful it'd happen. But what's to say it can't with Harry? Just because I'm asexual, it doesn't mean I can't have romance.

And Harry's already noticed me. Sure, I'll let him know I'm ace—the last thing I want to do is string him along and give him false expectations—and then I've just got to make sure he *keeps* noticing me after I tell him. I have to become the irresistible girl—one he may just be able to fall in love with and navigate an ace/allo relationship with.

A reminder pops up on my Facebook—his birthday is soon. Four days' time. I take a deep breath. Part of me is shocked I forgot it. I used to worship him even more on that day. Harry could be stuck at Goldwater then, if the lockdown isn't lifted. At the moment, we don't even know how long we'll be in lockdown.

I should get him a present. The idea comes to me all of a sudden. He can't be happy at the thought of spending his birthday stuck here. Maybe he'd been planning to meet up with family and friends after he'd done his journalism work that day. And he can't if the terrorists are still at large.

Yes, a present is a good idea.

Harry always liked bow ties. I remember that from school. When we were doing a project, he mentioned his preference for bow ties—I'm not sure why—and that he likes reptiles. He saw a bow tie with crocodiles on it in a charity shop once, and t back for it, but it had gone.

I hop onto Amazon and order a bow tie with little crocodiles on it. Delivery is apparently within two days, thanks to the Amazon Prime that I keep forgetting to cancel before it takes the next month's payment, but I don't even know whether couriers are still operating at the moment—not for non-essential items anyway. Still, the lockdown can't last for long, and the bow tie will get here at some point.

SIX

Harry

THE BASS PRACTICALLY *shakes the house.*

"Great party," Matt says, his arm around some blond girl I don't know.

It's a busy party, that's for sure. Crowded. So many people I don't know have turned up.

"Hey, Polly!" I shout.

I see her by the front door. Think she's just arrived. She doesn't look comfortable in here, and I think she's stretching up, trying to catch sight of one of her friends. Brooke and Brad are upstairs, in my room, but I saw Clare out on the patio not long ago, chugging back cans of beer, in a competition with some of the football guys.

I push past people, trying to devise a way through the crowd, to reach Polly. Wow, she looks good. She's got her hair down for once, and it's long and sleek. Never realized just how long it is. She's got a cute dress on. Blue and white flowery pattern. Her eyes are bright as she scans the room, and I don't know if she heard me, but—

"There you are," another voice says, and I turn to find Megan, captain of the dance team. She's all blond hair and red lipstick and, wow, that's one hell of a push-up bra.

Megan presses her lips to mine before I can do anything. She tastes of cheap beer, but her hands are roaming over my body. And Megan knows me. She knows what I like, how my body reacts.

She pulls at my arm, tugging me toward the stairs. There's a glint in her eyes that tells me everything about what she has planned for upstairs. And I may not be into her romantically, but right now, I sure am sexually.

I follow her, but not without one last look at Polly. And it's the moment when Polly turns and sees me being led away by Megan.

Hurt flashes across Polly's face, and I can't stop thinking about the look on her face for the rest of the night.

SEVEN

Polly

"DON'T ASK ANY really personal questions," Mum warns me as we walk up the drive to Fran and Ivan's house.

Gravel crunches under my feet. "Of course not."

I mean, I can't believe we're actually here. Last night was crazy. That party, seeing Harry go upstairs with Megan…again. I arrived home in tears, and of course Mum and Dad wanted to know why.

I told her how I liked a boy but that he'd never like me. And the whole being ace thing just spilled out because of course that's the reason Harry won't like me. It was the first time I'd mentioned it to anyone other than my close friends, and I was terrified.

And sure, Dad didn't get it. But Mum did.

"Yes, that's what Fran is," she said.

And I couldn't believe it. Fran, her work colleague, is asexual. Apparently, she's talked about her relationship with an allo man to my mum many a time. And Mum never mentioned it before—why would she? She didn't know I was ace too.

But now she does, and now we're here after a quick text message this morning.

A Black woman about ten years older than me opens the door, and Mum greets her with a loud, "Fran! How are you?"

I smile and stare at Fran as she exchanges greetings with my mum. For some reason, I'd expected her to be older. Closer to my mum's age.

"Come on in then," Fran says. She's wearing a light blue sun dress, and it clinches in at the waist emphasizing just how skinny she is. Her dark hair is pulled back in a high pony-tail with a bright red scrunchie that I see as she steps to the side and ushers me past into her house.

And what a house! It's modern and what Mum calls chic.

"Ivan's through there," Fran says, pointing to a doorway.

Through it, I find a bright and airy lounge with a leather three-piece suite. A man—Ivan—is sitting on the sofa, stroking a tabby cat. He smiles brightly as he sees me and Mum.

"You must be Polly." His smile is contagious. "I'm Ivan."

We shake hands, and then Fran's bringing in cups of tea—she must've just boiled the kettle before we arrived.

"So, your mum said you wanted to chat about being ace?" Fran smooths out her dress as she sits, then crosses one leg elegantly over the other.

"And about how you two manage a…relationship." Mum nearly whispers the last word. "Because Polly's said she's only going to look at dating other ace people, but you're the only one I know, and I'm worried she's not going to meet anyone whom she could have a relationship with…who's also like her."

Fran laughs. "It's perfectly possible to have a relationship with a man who isn't ace." She nods at Ivan. "I've done it. I'm not just limited to asexual men—you're right, there are way fewer of them. And what are the chances of meeting one in a place like this and getting on really well? No, Polly, don't rule out dating allos. It makes it more complicated, sure, dating one of them. But it doesn't mean an ace and allo can't be in love."

"And we're very much in love," Ivan says. His gaze has been on Fran the whole time she was speaking and even now he doesn't look away.

I look around and notice all the photos of the two of them on the mantelpiece. Fran and Ivan on a beach. A wedding photo. Them both riding a camel.

"I'm just worried Polly's going to get hurt." Mum takes a polite sip of her tea—a tiny little gulp. Nothing like the chugs she does back home, gulping back her Twinings. "This is all so new to her."

It's not new to me—I want to say it but I don't. But I've known since I was fourteen at least. It just took me years to tell anyone. And Brooke was the first to know.

"Then perhaps you need to focus on yourself for now, Polly," Fran says. "Take some time to understand what being ace means for you."

"I'm just worried she won't find love," Mum says. "I don't want her to be miserable and alone." She glances at me sideways.

"She won't be alone," Ivan says.

"So have you got any tips for when she's dating men who aren't...ace," Mum asks, and I can see she's trying so hard to help, but this whole thing is just incredibly embarrassing. I can't even believe Fran and Ivan are okay with this. I mean, isn't taking your daughter to your colleague who shares the same sexuality, to discuss said sexuality and dating, majorly creepy?

"We discussed expectations early on," Fran says, eyes on me. "And what a relationship meant for each of us. It's important to communicate—I mean, there's no easy way to lead into a conversation where you come out like that as ace, but it's got to be done. I always found early on was better too. Ivan was my third boyfriend. The first two were allo as well, but I hesitated in telling them. And the longer it went on, the harder I found it to talk about it. Like I'd been carrying this huge secret and it was just getting bigger. One of the blokes said he could change me—that was when I knew to kick him to the curb."

Ivan nods to Fran. "I appreciated being told about your sexuality straight away. I'll admit at first that I didn't really know what asexuality *was like. I remember on that same date—the first date, wasn't it?—I asked you if it was just a phase."*

"And I told you exactly what I thought of that!" Fran gives him a stern look, then laughs.

Ivan laughs—a throaty, genuine sound that oozes warmth. The cat gets up and stretches, before curling back up next to him. He strokes its back. "But Fran explained it to me, told me what it meant for her, and, well, I was already in love with her. I wasn't going anywhere. So, we just had to find a way to make it work that we were both happy with."

I glance at my Mum. I want to ask more specifically about the sex— whether that's part of the compromise the ace partner usually has to make in ace/allo relationships—but I feel heat flooding my face just thinking about asking them this question. And with my mum present too. Maybe if it was just Fran…

Instead, I nod and listen intently. But as luck would have it, Ivan volunteers the information.

"We decided which forms of intimacy were okay," he says. "Well, okay with Fran, because anything would've been okay for me." He laughs. "But respecting her decisions was the most important thing. And this man can live without sex." He points to himself, kind of dramatically. "And many allos understand that aces are out there. That not everything is about sex for everyone. For me it was about finding love. And I found it with Fran. Love is stronger than sex."

"But…" Mum looks around nervously, then clears her throat. "Is it reasonable to expect a partner who isn't asexual to be faithful if there is no sex? Because I don't want to Polly getting hurt—and this seems like it could make her very…vulnerable."

"Firstly, having sex with others doesn't always mean the person's not faithful," Fran says. "Many ace people with allo partners have an open relationship so their partner can get their sexual needs met that way. Plus,

there's also the option of poly relationships too. Neither open nor poly would have worked for me, and they don't work for all aces, but both are possibilities and there's nothing wrong with them."

Mum is frowning. I can tell she's not on board with this.

"If it's just sex, and the ace person is okay with it, and agrees to the allo partner going elsewhere for it, it's often fine," Fran continues.

"I don't want Polly getting cheated on," Mum says.

"Open and poly relationships aren't cheating," Fran stresses.

"I don't think that would work for me either though," I say. I know I'd get jealous. I wouldn't want to share Harry. Or anyone else I fall in love with. I'd be too worried all the time—because while sex doesn't really mean anything for me, I'd know that it does for an allo partner. He could fall in love with whoever he's sleeping with. I wouldn't be able to live happily with that constant worry.

"And that's fine," Fran says. "There are plenty of options. If you're interested in someone, be up front about your sexuality and what it means for you—because it is all individual. Some aces have sex to feel close to a partner, some are sex-repulsed. Some allo partners are satisfied with masturbation. Never feel any shame or anything regarding your thoughts and feelings on sex. And don't let anyone else shame you. It's just all about communication. And, girl, you've got nothing to worry about. You'll find someone."

I smile, even though this is the most embarrassing thing my mum's ever done, bringing me here to the only ace/allo couple she knows.

We talk a little more, mainly about online groups that Fran recommends I join, as well as something called AVEN.

On the way out, Fran passes me a scrap of paper. On it is a phone number.

"In case you've got any questions you don't want to ask in front of your mum," she says with a warm smile. "But it'll be okay, you're not alone,

You're not broken. You're just one of us."

EIGHT

Polly

HARRY IS WAITING by the black truck when I get there the next morning. The coming day is going to be hot—it may be just before seven, but the air's got that sticky quality already and there's not a cloud in the sky. It's going to turn into one of those postcard days.

"Hey, Polly." Harry's eyes brim with warmness. "I can't believe it's you. This is just…"

"Yeah, what are the chances?" I shoulder the bag Lisa had left out for me at the office. It's bulky with a tranquilizer gun sticking out of it. Late last night, she emailed us all with the extra precautions we've got to take now the county is in lockdown. We're all to patrol in twos, make sure that we've got fully charged mobiles and radios with us, as well as the tranquilizer guns that we'd normally only use on our animals that need veterinary attention. Of course, Lisa also said not to shoot the terrorists, should we see them, but we need to make sure we can defend ourselves if need be.

"So have you worked here since school?" he asks.

"Went to uni first. Then…" Then I was jobhunting for a year or so with no luck…then I had some time off. A year or so. After my parents and brother died. "Yeah, pretty much since then," I say. "What about you?"

"Yeah, done various internships at newspapers. I'm now writing for *Word Zero*. Based in London. Boss is a bit mean though. And God forbid if she hasn't had her morning coffee. One time, the coffee machine broke. I thought she was going to breathe fire or something."

I smile because it's so easy talking to Harry—I'd forgotten just how effortless it was. And then, of course, all my nerves come flooding back. About telling him I'm ace and seeing if a relationship is still possible. But no, I can do this. I've just got to make sure Harry keeps noticing me, even once I tell him.

And he'll be okay about it. Won't he?

I mean, this is assuming he's even interested in me at all anyway.

"Okay, let's get in." I unlock the truck and jump into the driver's seat.

Harry smiles as he climbs in next to me. "Wow, that is one overweight cat," he says, pointing to where Moggie is sort of sitting, sort of lying, nearby. She lifts her head up and watches us with her always-stern eyes. Every time I see her, I swear she's fatter.

The truck's engine rumbles to life, and we set off. I point out the different parts of Goldwater as we drive through them.

"Up there is where we get the most trouble with poachers." I nod ahead to the northern part of the grounds. It's more rugged and the edge of the woods is in sight. The fences on that side of the reserve keep falling down as the ground's not as stable, soft and squishy in places. And we haven't got the money to get the modern fences all around the park, not just yet. Not when we rely on visitor donations.

Donations that won't be forthcoming at the moment, not with no visitors. But this lockdown can't last long. That's what the article said that I read this morning as I chewed my bran flakes in the canteen—half looking out for Harry, who didn't appear.

I tap the steering wheel absentmindedly, drumming my fingers as I scan the area, you know, just in case some (or all) of the most wanted men are in fact hiding here. I find Harry is leaning toward me, peering at the ring on my right hand. The black band on my middle finger.

"It's an ace ring," I say, because it's easier just to get that out in the open. It's not like I put it on especially for this though; I always wear it.

"An ace ring?" Harry looks at me questioningly.

"Asexuality," I say. "I'm on the ace spectrum." My voice wavers, wobbles, and butterflies fill me. This is it… No going back now.

"Okay." His voice sounds strange, and I glance at him. "So, like… plants?"

"Plants?" I stare at him, mildly irritated as that's what a lot of people joke about as soon as asexuality is mentioned, but then I realize he looks sincere. "No. I'm not a plant. Asexuality means not feeling sexual attraction or having sexual feelings. I'm still a person."

Harry swallows visibly, his Adam's apple bobbing up and down. I focus back on the road, feel heat rushing to my face. He doesn't understand it. Oh, God. What was I thinking, believing that an ace/allo relationship with him would be possible? Brooke was right. Hell, maybe even my mum was right to be worried. Maybe Fran and Ivan are the exception.

"That's cool," Harry says at last.

"Cool?" I drive a little faster, wanting this tour to be over with.

"Yeah, I mean, everyone's open to all these different identities now." He frowns.

"Well, that's the eastern border there," I say, glad to get back to the tour. "See the buildings over there? The ones like tents? They're the hides."

Harry's still frowning when I glance over at him. Staring straight ahead at the hides and frowning.

"They're for watching wildlife," I say.

"I know." Still frowning.

"What is it?" I ask, slowing the truck down.

"I'm just surprised—and I feel incredibly stupid now." He looks over to me, and his eyes are bright and earnest.

"Why?" I stop the truck and look at him. He looks genuinely worried and embarrassed—both at the same time.

"Well, last night, I thought…when I came out from the shower…and that text I sent. I didn't mean to make you uncomfortable."

I smile. "You didn't. Honestly."

"No wonder you barely said a word to me." He shakes his head.

"I was just…surprised to see you. Plus, you do look good in a towel." I give him another grin.

Now he frowns. "You think I look good in a towel, *yet* you're asexual?"

I want to roll my eyes. "Sexual attraction isn't the only type of attraction. There's emotional, physical, aesthetic attraction too. And more." I've thought for a long time I should get a T-shirt printed with this info on. "So I can want to touch someone and have emotional intimacy, and a deep connection, but it doesn't mean I want to have sex."

Harry breathes out slowly. "So long as I didn't offend you or anything?"

"You didn't. Don't worry."

"How long have you been like this?" he asks.

Been like this… I grimace at his wording.

"How long have you been allo?" I ask.

"Allo?"

"Opposite to ace. Because I assume you're not on the asexual spectrum?"

He smiles. "Touché. Sorry, I'm just… I hadn't really heard of asexuality before this. It's all new. So, are you just like…friends with any partners then? But not like romantic?"

I snort. "I can't speak for all of us. We're all different. Some like romance, some don't. And I do feel romantic attraction. So, no, it's not *just* about being really good friends. And even those who are aro—that's aromantic, by the way—probably wouldn't appreciate you saying that it's *just* about being friends with a partner—like, saying 'just' sort of diminishes the importance of the relationship."

Fran knows a couple aro-aces and shortly after I met her, she introduced me to them. They described their relationships as intense and personal, more than a close friend, even if there was no romance or sex.

Harry is frowning. "Sorry if this is insensitive, Polly, but I don't get it. How is it any different from a friend, if you don't have sex? Like, even with romance?"

"Okay, so Brooke's my best friend. But I don't want to lie in bed, cuddling her. I don't want to kiss her and give her massages. I don't want sensual intimacy from her. And we don't do romantic things for each other, or plan lives together—even if we happen to be roommates right now."

"So it's like a relationship, but without the sex?"

"It *is* a relationship," I correct.

Harry nods. And he doesn't say anything else for the rest of the patrol, just listens as I show him the remaining part of the nature reserve and the farming unit.

I pace round and round my room at lunch, can't bear the thought of getting food at the canteen. Where Harry is. Not that I could stomach food right now.

This plan was a bad idea. What was I thinking, believing that I could come out to Harry and then expect him to still be interested? I was just kidding myself. Even if he may have been flirting with me before.

Because that's definitely not going to happen now. And no amount of actions to make him notice me is going to make him fall in love with me. Declaring my asexuality has put up walls between us. But it's better that we both discovered the extent of the walls now, rather than later...

Who am I kidding? Maybe he wouldn't have been interested in me even if I was allo?

"Are you going to stop that? You're making me dizzy." Brooke groans. She's sitting by her desk, a dozen spreadsheets printed out in front of her. She pulls on her hair as she looks at the photo of her family. It was taken by me last Christmas. Every fifth year since Brooke was a baby, the Taiwanese side of her family visits England and they celebrate together, with Brooke's parents, Shu-li and James, and then James's family drives down for Boxing Day too. Last year, the Kaos visited again, and I'd been apprehensive as to how I'd fit into the picture. I was sort of used to spending Christmas with Brooke, her parents, and two brothers, following the arrangements made in the years since my family passed, and I was nervous. But Hsiao-han, Brooke's maternal grandmother, had welcomed me with every ounce of her being. Brooke had told them before they arrived that I'd be there, and what had happened to my family, and Hsiao-han had brought gifts for me too: calligraphy pens and facemasks.

"Sorry." I force myself to sit down, then check my phone for any email from the dating holiday company. Nothing. I groan. Going to have to phone to see if I can get my deposit back. Only I hate phoning…

I feel like screaming, because of that and because of Harry.

Harry.

No! I need to try to distract myself. I'm working a maintenance shift with Grant in half an hour. Repairing some of the fences up in the poacher range. Well, repairing them as best as we can without proper materials.

I run a hand through my hair. How expensive can those materials be?

I grab my laptop, open Safari. And Facebook automatically loads.

Mustn't have closed the browser properly last time. And now Harry's profile picture fills the screen. He's updated it. *Of course* he looks good.

I find myself navigating to his profile. Reading his updates, looking at his photos, his relationship status—single.

I close my laptop quickly. No point torturing myself even more.

NINE

Harry

POLLY'S *ASEXUAL*.

God. I feel stupid. How didn't I know? And why did I react like I did? Likening her to a freaking plant. Man, she's going to hate me. Never want to talk to me again.

I take a deep breath. I should've been nicer... God, was I really that bad? I hope I didn't come across as... what's the word for being phobic of asexual people?

I pull my phone out and Google it.

Acephobic.

Okay. I take a deep breath. The sun's beating its rays down on me and sweat drips down my back, sticking my shirt to me. I run a hand through my hair. I don't think I said anything really bad. I was just surprised, and I've never really met an asexual person. Well, not that I know of.

Somewhere nearby, a goat bleats.

And now there's Polly. Polly who used to be my best friend as a child.

Polly who I had the most massive crush on when I was eighteen.

Polly who's clever and kind.

Polly who's ace.

And I practically flashed her when I came out of the bathroom last night. I mean, she said it didn't offend her but I can't help but worry.

And when I saw her here the day I arrived, when I was sure it was Polly Brady, I was immediately wondering if she had a boyfriend. Wondering what it would be like to kiss her under the setting sun here at Goldwater.

And she's asexual. She's going to want an asexual partner.

"We've got to clean out the stables now," Evie calls over to me. And damn, I'd forgotten she was here. Or maybe she just got back—she keeps popping out to use the toilets. Said she's got some bladder condition or something. I'm on the mucking-out shift with her. Which means cleaning up all sorts of animal dung.

Alongside the bigger more industrial farm, Goldwater has a little petting farm at one side with pygmy goats, some Shetland ponies, and sheep. Polly told me earlier that much of the income comes from their 'experience days' where they offer members of the public the chance to 'be a farmer for a day'. This whole initiative was Evie's idea and she normally runs it all with day-time staff.

But now it's me helping her.

I grab a shovel and head into the nearest stable. And, dear God, I can smell the manure.

"Fresh, isn't it?" Evie laughs, following me. I turn to see she's got a wheelbarrow. "But it's a lot cooler in here."

It certainly is.

Evie keeps trying to engage me in conversation, but I don't feel like talking. Even if it is a distraction. I need to apologize to Polly. It must've been difficult enough telling me all that stuff, and then I reacted like that.

Oh no. I'm like the mean guy in some film.

No. I'm over-reacting, aren't I?

It wasn't that bad.

Was it?

But what if you'd *been telling her you were ace or something, and she'd gone all quiet?*

I swallow hard, can't get the thought of her out of my mind. And I know I should. I've got to concentrate. Aside from this manual work. I'm supposed to be preparing a report on Goldwater, ahead of the gala. I'm supposed to make the atmosphere sound lively and friendly and cheerful.

But the smell of goat feces isn't making me feel cheerful. Nor is the conversation with Polly earlier, with how I ended it. God, why did I go silent on her?

"Good job," Evie tells me some hours later, and I'm almost surprised by just how much time has passed. It's dinner time.

Dinner in the canteen.

Where Polly will be?

Evie and I walk there together. I think she keeps batting her lashes at me, and I notice she's wearing makeup. I haven't seen any of the other women here—Polly included—wearing much makeup. Doesn't seem like a practical place to. And I'm pretty sure Evie wasn't dolled up like this yesterday. I'd have noticed that—the purple lipstick and sparkly stuff on her eyelids.

"You coming in?" Evie asks. "Think it's shepherd's pie tonight. Or there's a veggie version. Are you vegetarian?"

"No." I shake my head.

"So, are you coming?"

"I'm just going to wait here," I tell Evie, and I watch her enter—albeit reluctantly—and I wait. And wait. And wait.

"Polly." I corner her as she's entering the canteen. I'd almost given up on seeing her, thinking she was eating elsewhere tonight, but she arrives at just gone eight.

She looks surprised to see me, and adjusts her ponytail, tightening it.

"I just want to say it's cool," I say.

"Cool?"

"You being ace."

"Me being ace?" She raises her eyebrows. "Well, uh, thanks. But I don't need your approval."

And there it is. I know I've hurt her.

"I didn't mean it like that—and I didn't mean to go all quiet. I was just…processing it."

"Processing?" She frowns, then looks up at me. The light in her eyes has changed. "What is there to process?"

"I don't know."

Just that I really like you. And it means a lot to me that you told me.

But, of course, I don't say it. I'm too chicken, as Bo would say.

Polly and I step to the side to let Lisa and Grant into the canteen, and it puts my body in close proximity to Polly's. I can smell the faint aroma of her shampoo. Every part of me wants to reach out and brush a hand along her face, just to touch her. But I can't.

I don't know if she'd like it, if it would even be okay. She said she likes romance and intimacy, but that doesn't just mean I can touch her uninvited.

But it doesn't stop feelings—things—stirring in me.

"It's okay, honestly," she says. "You getting food?"

"Yeah, I guess." I follow her into the canteen, see her wave at Brooke. Brooke—who I'm sure is glaring at me. She never liked me at school. She only just about tolerated me.

Polly starts talking to me about the latest movie she's watched, and she's chattering away, her voice all light, and I don't think she's angry with me at all. I mean, she seems to want to talk to me. So that's good.

"Come and sit with us," she says, heading over to where Brooke's still glaring at me.

"Uh," I say. "Is Brooke okay with that?" My tray of food seems to get heavier.

"Brooke's just being Brooke," she says. "And you're—"

"Poachers!" someone yells.

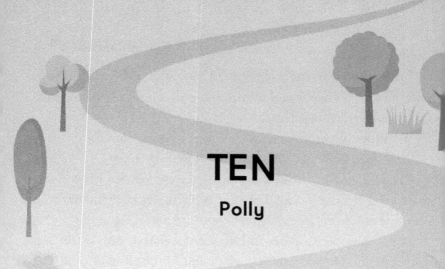

TEN
Polly

"POACHERS!" THE SHOUT rings out through the canteen.

Immediately, the other rangers and I spring into action. We sprint out of the canteen and jump into vehicles. I'm in the passenger seat of the black truck, next to Grant who takes the wheel. The doors behind us slam shut, and in the rear-view mirror I see that Evie and Harry are in the back. Evie's got her radio out and she's talking to Jane, Lisa, and Morris in the other vehicle. And why in the world has Harry jumped in the truck for this?

"Do we know where they are?" Grant asks, putting his foot down. The vehicle lurches forward—its acceleration is never smooth.

"Over to the west side," Evie says. "Lisa's got the police on the line. What if they're the terrorists?"

"Won't be," Grant shouts.

"So, what are we doing?" Harry asks.

"Detaining them until the cops get here," I say as terrain flies past the windows.

"But isn't that dangerous?" And bless him, he actually sounds worried.

"They'll take our deer otherwise." I shrug and look around and ahead. "There!"

I see them. A group of four or five men, all with rifles and hunting guns. They're crouching in the undergrowth, and they've seen us, that's clear. I scan the area. Can't see any animals with them. Dead or alive.

"Evie, tell Jane to drive over to the west side of the trees," I say.

My heart pounds and adrenaline races through my system. There's a rushing sound in my ears, so much so I can't make out Evie's words as she radios the other truck. This is pure thrill, this energy.

"They're moving!" I yell, just as two of the poachers try and make a run for it, back to the fence. "Go!"

"Camera's running!" Evie shouts.

Grant puts his foot down and the wheels spin dust all around us as we race around, halting to a stop in front of the two poachers.

They stop, stare at us. Both of these are young men we've seen here before. I'm surprised—last I saw of them, a couple months ago, they were leaving Goldwater in the back of a police van. And then suddenly my brain's doing crazy things— making me think Evie is right and that these could actually *be* two of the terrorists. And they're *here* and...

No. They're poachers. I know these two men. And they look nothing like the mugshots that have been circulating.

"Now," I yell, and Grant and I both throw our doors open and jump out.

Evie's behind us, with the camera.

I run toward the men. "Put your weapons down," I yell. Behind them, the other two are still crouched in the trees. And beyond them, Lisa, Morris, and Jane are approaching. "You're under arrest." We have the power to detain them until the cops get here.

The two men nearest me look at each other.

"Get out of my way," one snarls, taking a step toward me. He points his gun at me.

My heart pounds. It's all just bravado. They wouldn't shoot us—not with so many of us and a camera rolling. And these two know we always call the cops. All the poachers must, even those we've not caught before. We put out enough publicity about the evil work of poachers. 'Stop the Poachers' is one of our biggest annual campaigns.

"I mean it," the poacher shouts. "Get out of my way now. You're going to let us go."

"No," I say, trying to keep my voice calm. But I haven't got my dart gun on me. It's in the truck. "We are not."

"Polly, get back," Grant hisses.

But I don't get back.

I stand my ground. I'm not scared of these men.

The poacher takes a step toward me. "You're going to regret this."

I start to smile. Sirens, in the distance. "You're not winning this. Police are on their way and—"

And a lot of things happen at once.

The poacher takes another step toward me, his gun definitely on me. Harry screams my name, and Grant and Lisa are shouting.

And the poacher fires his gun at me.

ELEVEN
Polly

A WEIGHT HITS me as the poacher's gun goes off, and I'm knocked to the ground. Dust in my mouth, and I bite the insides of my cheeks. Hot pain unleashes through me as I roll away from whatever it was that hit me and—

Harry. He's right next to me, lying down.

He was what hit me.

He threw himself at me. Into the line of gunfire.

"Put the weapons down!" Grant shouts, and then Lisa and Evie are shouting it too. And Lisa's got her tranquilizer gun out.

"Polly, are you okay?" Harry reaches out for me, brushes his fingers against my face. He's shaking, and his touch is like electricity.

I jolt, staring into his deep eyes. My breaths sound strange, too fast, too heavy. "Yeah."

He's got dirt smudged on his face, and his clothes. And it's like time stops with just the two of us—even though I'm aware of everything else going on, how the poachers are surrendering, how the sirens are getting nearer, how Grant is getting the ropes out to bind the men's hands. But all I can focus on is Harry.

Right next to me. His fingers are still on my face, and I've never seen that look in his eyes—a protective look.

Protective of me.

He threw himself into gunfire for me.

I swallow hard, feel strange.

"Are you sure you're okay?" Harry asks.

"Yeah. Uh, I better help them." I gesture toward Grant and Lisa.

"Okay." Harry jumps up and offers me a hand.

I take it, and his touch is still electrifying, leaves me giddy and breathless. This is Harry Weller helping me up. Trying to save my life.

And he did save it. The poacher shot *at* me.

"Take Polly back to the village," Grant shouts, and he tosses the keys of the black truck at Harry who catches them deftly. Of course he does.

"No, I'm fine," I say.

Grant shakes his head.

I want to argue—really want to. But I look around and I can see they've got it all sorted now. Not to mention the sirens are louder. Brooke will be at the main gates to let the police into the grounds.

"Come on," Harry says. He offers me his hand for a second time.

I take it.

"You just jumped straight in there, Polly," Harry says. He blinks several times. We're in the canteen. He got two hot chocolates from the vending machine, but they're both sitting untouched on the table between us. "Those men had guns."

"I know," I say. "They don't normally shoot. Must be desperate."

"You could've been seriously hurt." He reaches out, touches my arm. "Or worse."

"I'm okay," I say, hardly daring to breathe because Harry is touching me again. His hand on me sends tingles through me, and I want to cuddle up with him, have his arms around me as he cradles me close to his heart.

He's right. I'm shaken by the events now. Now I've had time to process it and the adrenaline's dying away.

Harry smiles, but there's a depth to it that shows he's not happy. Maybe relieved, but worried and concerned too. He slides his hand down my arm, to my wrist, then my hand. He squeezes my fingers.

"Thank you," I whisper.

"You don't need to thank me."

"You saved my life."

He nods a little, then squeezes my hand tighter. "I didn't want you to die."

I didn't want you to die. I mull over the words. Does that mean there is something between us? And that he feels it too? Or did he really just do what he would for anyone? If it had been Grant, would he have thrown himself into harm's way?

But if he did, I can't imagine him sitting in the canteen with Grant, holding his hand.

There is something between me and Harry. He has to feel it too.

TWELVE

Harry

I CAN'T SLEEP. Every time I close my eyes, I'm back there. Watching the poacher take his aim at Polly. Only this time, I'm not quick enough. I sprint toward her, forcing every ounce of energy into my speed—but it's not enough.

The bullet hits her. She falls. Blood. An explosion of it, over me.

Death.

And Polly—gone. Lying in my arms, soundless, unmoving.

It's like a blow to the stomach each time, and I gulp, feeling sick.

Polly could've died.

Hell, I could have too—and it's the first time I realize I risked my own life. But I had to. To save her.

Because I like her. I've always liked her.

And seeing her again made me think that maybe we are supposed to end up together.

Only she's asexual.

I take a deep breath.

She's still Polly.

Being asexual doesn't mean she's not the girl I grew up with, the girl I worked with on history projects, the girl I wished I was kissing—and doing more with—at parties.

Only she's not going to want to do more.

I groan.

I grab my phone from where it lies next to me on my pillow. I need to learn more about asexuality. I need to know if there's a way it could work between us. Polly mentioned other types of chemistry before—and holding her hand in the canteen, she had to feel that energy then, right?

THIRTEEN

Harry

"WHERE'VE YOU BEEN?" Bo blocks the doorway. Of course, I'm trying to sneak through it, hoping no one has noticed how late I've been out.

But of course my brother has noticed. Since Dad died, he's taken on the role of Man of the House. He knows everything about me and Sara, it seems: where we are, who we're with, and what we're doing. Except tonight, apparently. Bo looks worried.

"Have you any idea what time it is?" Bo gives me the stern look that just makes him look more like Dad.

"Sorry, I was studying at the park."

"Studying?" Bo raises his eyebrows. "At this time? Harry, it's nearly midnight. It's dark."

"I was *studying*."

"Who with?"

"Polly," I say, and I remember how the scent of shampoo—coconut—drifted over me. We sat by the river and worked on our project until it got dark and Polly was cold. But she didn't want to go home then, that was clear. Mum heard something about the Bradys having marital problems. A couple of times, Polly's arrived at school tear-stained and I couldn't help but notice that neither of her parents came to the latest parents' evening. That was the first time it happened. Instead, Polly's brother Cameron went with her. When I walked past them, as they were waiting for their appointment with Polly's tutor, I heard Cameron consoling Polly. Something that sounded like, "Dad doesn't mean all that he's saying to Mum."

"Polly?" Bo frowns. "That scrappy kid from down the road?"

"She's not scrappy," I say, and it annoys me hearing Bo talk about Polly like that. Sure, we've known Polly for years, ever since the two of us were little, when Polly's family moved down here.

Bo was friends with her brother until they went to different secondary schools. And me and Sara played with Polly, having water fights in the summer, going to the cinema together, eating ice cream at Easter because Sara's allergic to chocolate and so we always made the day after Easter, when we were allowed away from our families, our designated Ice Cream Day. It was a tradition we kept up for three years, until Polly's family moved to the other side of town.

Now Bo raises his eyebrows. "You expect me to believe you were studying?"

"We were," I say. "Look, you can see the work we did."

I pull out my history book from my bag. It's pure luck that today's the one day I've got it instead of Polly. For the last month, she's looked after it—the ongoing joint project that's due at the end of term for extra credit. But when we were trying to work out how to incorporate more statistics into the work, she knocked over her water bottle and it soaked her bag and everything inside it. So I took the work home today instead.

"So you worked even though it's pitch-black outside. You expect me to believe this?"

Now my patience is getting thin. I'm tired. "Look, we worked until it got dark. Then we walked around a bit. And I walked Polly home, before heading here. Added an hour onto my walk."

Bo grunts. "Just get to bed and don't wake up Mum."

FOURTEEN

Polly

"SO, I LOOKED up asexuality," Harry tells me the next morning as he sits down at the table with me and Brooke for breakfast. "And it's confusing as hell."

"Uh, not really." I frown. "But good morning to you too. Sleep well? Do you want any—"

Brooke cuts me off with a snort, a glare directed at Harry. "You wouldn't say *your* sexuality is confusing as hell. And yet I bet five men who all identify the same way you do will all have different likes. Like, how much sex they prefer, how much romance, how easily it is for them to get aroused."

Though last night Brooke wouldn't stop gushing about how Harry saved me, now she's only emitting cold vibes in his direction. She's worried for me, that's clear.

"Good point." Harry nods, though I'm sure he's uncomfortable with the bluntness of Brooke's words. "I... I think it's all these names. I haven't heard of them before." He looks down at his phone and taps for a few seconds. "Gray-ace, demi, aromantic, heteromantic, homoromantic, flux... I can't remember what that is. And there's the whole sex-repulsion thing as well..." He looks bewildered. "*I'm* finding it confusing."

"You don't need to." I'm smiling. I can see the screen of his phone—and he's made notes on this in the notes app. A warm feeling fills me.

"So, what are you then?" He frowns slightly as he looks at me, and the look is so cute on him.

"Heteromantic," I say. "That's what I generally go with. For a while, I thought I was demi—but even when I formed a strong emotional connection with someone, I wasn't interested in sex." I mean, at the time I thought it was because I wasn't as in love with Peter, as I was with Harry, but prior to sex, Peter and I did have a strong bond, even so. Yet engaging in sex had pretty much removed any feelings I'd had for him. And even now, looking at Harry, I can't imagine myself *wanting* to have sexual contact with him—even though I know I already love him. And I don't want to have sex because I know it'll change things for me, change my feelings for him. I just want to cuddle with him in bed, and press my skin against his, and feel his arms around me. Have a deep connection.

"Are you sex-repulsed?" Harry asks.

"That is an awfully personal thing to ask, you know," Brooke tells him. "Just because she's ace, it doesn't mean she's got to answer loads of really private questions. It's not her job to educate you."

He blushes. "I'm sorry. Oh, God, I even saw that on a forum last night—some girl saying that aces aren't there to teach allos about ace stuff."

It sounds weird, hearing him use the terms *ace* and *allo*. But it also gives me a warm feeling. Because he's trying, isn't he? I mean, he *researched* asexuality. He's been reading forums.

"It's okay," I say. "Because I know you. But don't think you can ask *any* ace person this."

"Got it." He nods. He makes direct eye contact. Then he smiles, flashing ever so slightly crooked teeth at me. "So, heteromantic. Got it."

"*Got it?* What the hell's that supposed to mean?"

"It means *stop all this right now*," Brooke says. "Just ignore his flirting. You're only going to get hurt."

I stare at her. We're walking to the truck. Time for the first patrol of the day. We're doing them more frequently now since yesterday with the poachers. And I double check I've got the tranquilizer gun. "You don't think aces and allos can have relationships."

"I do," she says. "And I only want what's best for you. I don't want Harry to break your heart. And I don't even know how you can think about romance right now—we're in lockdown. Actual terrorists are hiding somewhere in Devon."

"But Harry and I could make it work."

She gives me a level look. "Pols, you and I both know how much he likes sex. Sure, he could agree to give it up. Or I don't know, you compromise or something. But what if whatever you decide isn't enough for him? He could leave you, when you're completely in love with him—like even more than you are right now."

"That's a risk in any relationship."

"But it's more of a risk in one such as this, I'm sure. And I'm only saying this because you're my best friend and I love you."

"I know," I say.

She reaches out and squeezes my arm. "We'll find you an ace guy."

The internet's not always that strong at Goldwater, but Facetime works enough for Fran's face to fill the screen. The moment Brooke left our room to go and get a coffee after her evening shift, I called Fran. Like I always do when it comes to matters of the heart. Even when my parents were alive, it was always Fran I called about my love life. We kept in contact after that first visit when Mum took me to see her. And when my family was killed, Fran and Ivan took me in for a while. Just until I got my head sorted and Brooke got this job arranged for me.

Fran, Ivan, and Brooke (and the rest of the Kaos) are my family now.

"So, this is the Harry Weller from school?" she asks. She's got minimal make up on today, and she looks more beautiful than ever.

"Yeah, it's him. And he saved me when a poacher tried to shoot me. And I think he likes me. He's looked up all about asexuality and asked me if I'm romantic and sex-repulsed."

"Well, good communication is a strong start," Fran says.

"But Brooke thinks it can only end in disaster. When we were at school, he slept with a lot of girls. He had, like, this huge reputation. I mean, he was in the popular crowd, but still. So, I don't know if it can work. I mean… I know you and Ivan do, but I don't know whether it's even an option for me and Harry"

Fran gives me a stern look. "You need to talk to him. *I* can't tell you whether it'll work. That's something only the two of you can decide. You just need to ask him all this. You need to talk. Like I said, it's all about communication."

The door creaks open. It's Brooke, returning.

"I know, but…" I run my hands through my hair. "It's awkward saying it."

"But it's got to be done, if you're going to try this. And," she adds, "you've got to try this, Polly. I know you, girl, and I know you'll regret it if you don't."

I glance at Brooke. She's watching me with her lips pressed together in a very thin line, but then waves to Fran.

"Girls, I've got to go now, but just listen to what your heart says. I listened to mine, and I was right to get together with Ivan—even though I had reservations at first about whether it could work."

"You did?" I stare at her. She and Ivan just seem so in-tune and compatible, I can't ever imagine Fran having doubts.

"Yeah, about much the same thing as you. It's the sex. The difference in our needs that bothered me. That he'd think I was leading him on, or believe I'd change my mind eventually. But we found a way around the sex issue—and it wasn't even as big a deal as I'd been thinking it was. I mean, there are always ways around it."

"So, you think Polly should have an open relationship?" Brooke frowns. "Because, Polly, isn't that going to hurt you? I know you and you'll worry that sex with someone else will lead Harry to love them more than you."

"No," Fran says. "Open relationships aren't the only solution here, Brooke. Sex isn't just about *having* sex. And a man can take care of himself too, don't forget that too." She raises her eyebrows as she nods. "Now, I've really got to go, but speak soon, Polly."

When the call ends, silence fills our room, except for Brooke blowing the steam off her coffee. She takes a long sip.

"Well, come on then," Brooke says.

"What? Where?"

"Grant organized a pool tournament in the games room. Harry was talking about it earlier. We better get down there and let him know you're interested."

FIFTEEN

Polly

THE GAMES ROOM has to be the one room in the accommodation block that I rarely visit. It's in the basement and smells strongly of damp and beer—no matter how much cleaning or damp-proofing is done—and it tends to be where Grant, Evie, and Morris hang out. Sometimes Jane and George are there too. The basement is huge, spreading underneath the whole of the block, making it the biggest room by far. There's a pool table at one side, and then some old sofas on the other, near 'the bar,' which is just a table with beer bottles standing on it.

I wrinkle my nose at the smell as Brooke and I stand in the entrance. Rap music blares from a speaker, but I think it's being streamed because it keeps pausing for half a second before stuttering on.

Grant, Morris, and Harry are standing around the pool table. Evie's just behind them, sitting on a table, her skinny tan-lined legs crossed over each other. She looks up and sees me and Brooke and waves us over.

"Didn't know you were playing as well!" she says. "Hey, Morris, add Brooke and Polly to the scoreboard."

She indicates the whiteboard that's Duct-taped to the wall.

"It's okay, I'm not playing," I say.

"Then why are you here?" Evie frowns.

"I…" My mouth dries and I can feel Harry's full gaze on me. "Just to socialize."

Evie smiles and says something, but I don't catch it.

"We're gonna be over there," Brooke says, her eyes lingering on Harry for a second, then flicking toward me. She leads me over to the nicest of the sofas. It's only got a few stains on.

Carefully, I sit on the most unstained part. Brooke just plonks herself down, not checking the fabric. She pulls her phone out and checks the news for the latest reports on the manhunt. She's always liked true crime, and I suppose the county being in lockdown because wanted men are on the run fits into her interest. But she's taking this more seriously than I thought she would. When she's reading about true crime, she almost looks excited. But with this, she looks worried. Probably because it's close to home. This is real, happening now.

"I can't believe the speed at which this manhunt is moving at," she says. "You'd think they'd have found the terrorists by now. I mean, the police have got all this tech. And apparent sightings too. Must be understaffed. Or it's the budget cuts."

She's frowning. Out of all of us here—bar Evie on that first night—Brooke definitely seems the most worried.

"Probably," I say. And I wonder why I'm not feeling worried. Because it doesn't feel real? But if that poacher who shot at me had been one of the wanted men for the terror attacks how different would I be feeling now? Especially if they'd escaped and not been taken away by the cops. I'd be living on tenterhooks, jumping at my own shadow, constantly on guard.

I mean, I'm pleased I'm relaxed, but I almost feel too relaxed in the face of more possible attacks. Because these men are terrorists. They've done a string of knife attacks across the UK so far. What's to stop them from orchestrating another right now, especially if they know their time on the run is running out?

It's Harry being here that means I'm not taking this seriously—it has to be. I'm distracted by him.

"Look at this." Brooke shows me her phone. A photo of Exeter High Street fills it. It's completely deserted. The whole place looks ghostly. Like it's been forgotten, left behind. Brooke scrolls through more and more similar photos. "People really are obeying the lockdown, scared to go out. Not like how many of them disobeyed the lockdown when there was the coronavirus pandemic. I suppose being caught up in a terrorist attack is a more immediate threat of death than the virus."

"Do you think there will be another attack?" I ask her. So far, the attacks have been in other counties, mostly in the midlands and the north, as well as near London—though not actually in the capital city itself.

My skin crawls.

Brooke shrugs. "Either they will, as they want to be noticed. Or they're going to lie low until they can get out and disappear and—" She trails off as she sees Harry approaching us.

I sit up a bit straighter, suddenly feeling self-conscious.

"Hey," Harry says, giving me a smile that makes my heart melt. "You okay?"

"Yeah." I give him a nod.

Evie sidles over. "We were just discussing what we're going to do for Harry's birthday."

"What do you mean?" Brooke asks.

"Well, when it's one of our birthdays, we always do something," Evie says. "Some sort of celebration."

Brooke's eyes flick to Harry, then back to Evie. "Yeah, but he's not one of us."

"Hey, he is while we're all locked in here," Evie says, her tone so clearly protective and defensive.

"So what's the plan?" I ask. I think of my present for Harry and wonder if it will actually get here in time.

"Fancy dress." Harry covers up a laugh with a cough when Evie shoots one of her glares at him.

"It's a brilliant theme," she gushes.

"Fancy dress isn't really a theme though," I say.

Now, Evie shoots the glare at me.

"Let's make it whacky," Harry says. "Craziest costume gets a prize."

"Ah well I've already won then," I say, thinking about the one and only fancy dress costume I have in my wardrobe. It was my brother's. He ordered it as a joke, in the days before he died. It was custom made from a designer in the US, and it didn't arrive at our house until six weeks later. When I opened the box, I felt strange. Like I was prying into something that wasn't mine to see. I was a trespasser on the last actions of my brother.

The costume itself is hideous—but I couldn't get rid of it.

I put it on straight away. That was the first time. And then I wore it around the house a fair bit after that. Whenever I was feeling lonely and sad. That was until Fran and Ivan took me in for a little while. And then Brooke and her parents took over after that, when Ivan had a health scare and I didn't want to be intruding on him and Fran.

"Yeah, but you won't want that costume getting messed up," Brooke says, placing a hand on my shoulder.

Harry's eyes are inquisitive. "What is the costume?"

"You'll have to wait and see." I laugh. That costume will definitely make sure he keeps noticing me.

"Okay, back to the game," Evie says, and she steers Harry away.

"You know," Brooke says. "She comes across as kind of desperate, but really cute too. Like a fierce little frog or something." She sees the look on my face. "Don't worry. If Harry's into anyone here, it's you. Not her."

But Harry's now laughing throatily at something she says, and I watch his body language by the pool table as they wait for Morris to finish his turn. I see how Harry's leaning in toward Evie, how, after a few moments, he's fully focused on her.

She laughs and touches his arm, and then they're getting closer.

I glance at Brooke. She's watching them too, her eyes sharp. *If Harry's into anyone here, it's you. Not her.*

But I think Brooke's wrong. Evie's all over Harry now and he seems to be enjoying it. He's smiling and laughing and...touching her arm.

Just like he did with me. Only with her it's more—it's obvious.

He says something, and she laughs in a stupid high-pitched tone. And I realize as I watch them that he's never going to notice me in the way I want him to. Not when Evie's beautiful and blonde with a killer figure. And I'm just...ordinary.

And asexual.

SIXTEEN

Harry

"IT'S OKAY, MUM." I hold her hand and the dogs are pressing against her as her whole body shakes with tears.

From the doorway, Sara gives me an alarmed look, eyes all wide. In the kitchen, I can hear Bo's on the phone, reporting the crime to the police.

I look around the living room, suddenly wondering if we should even be in here. This is a crime scene. But I can't see Mum agreeing to move outside until the cops get here. She's just crying and gulping as she sits on the sofa, eyes staring straight forward at the place where Dad's collection should be.

I didn't get a clear glimpse of the men that broke in. Bo and I were out. We just got a panicked call from Sara.

"There was a man here and he pointed a gun at Mum."

We hurried back, hearts pounding, and found Mum and Sara in tears, speaking in jumbled sentences about men and firearms. The men who took Dad's collection of rare coins. The collection that he put his life and soul—literally—into. Dad died three years ago. He was traveling to Canada to look at some rare coin when he had a heart attack. He didn't return.

Now, all we have are his coins.

Or, rather, had.

I hear Bo end the phone call. "Police are on their way," he says. "It'll be okay."

His face is a picture of calmness. I've always envied my older brother of that ability, how he can seamlessly turn off his expressions. Replace them with a smooth curtain to reassure us. But I know my brother and he still feels deeply.

When Dad died, Bo didn't cry once in front of us. He was the practical one. He did most of the organization for the funeral. I'd have thought he wasn't affected at all, if I hadn't heard his sobs at night, through the wall we share.

Mum's eyes are glassy. She's still staring at the empty mantelpiece. I want to jump up and put something there, try and fill the empty space.

But some spaces can never be filled.

"He's gone," Mum says. "He's finally, completely gone." Her voice wavers. "You're gone, John. Gone. Go away."

I widen my eyes at Bo, that creeping feeling pulling through me again. Mum does this. She still sees Dad. Even though he's not there.

"Mum, it's okay," Sara says.

But Mum jumps up and there is fire in her eyes as she turns around. Sometimes, when she's like this, I think she's possessed. I know I shouldn't think that—she's not well. It started when Dad died. Grief. A mental breakdown.

But I get scared. And I shouldn't, because I'm nearly a man.

But I'm not the man of the house. That's Bo.

He walks calmly over to Mum, places his hands on her shoulders and guides her to rest her head against his chest. Bo's touch is always like magic.

"Don't be angry, John," Mum whispers. Her face is wet with tears and she curls her fingers into Bo's flannel shirt. "I did my best."

SEVENTEEN
Polly

THE NEXT MORNING, Harry and I are on ranger duty together again. Lisa emailed round another new schedule last night. Evie and Jane were out on patrol together yesterday, just as Brooke and I were in the morning, but Lisa now wants a man in every patrol pairing. I can't decide whether that's sexist or not. And when I saw I was paired with Harry again, I just stared at the text blankly, praying that by the time morning came, it would change.

It hasn't.

I get to the truck first, feeling sick. Harry's going to be here any moment, and he was flirting with Evie. He likes her. Not me.

It's a cliché, but I feel like my heart has fractured into a million fragments and each shard is piercing my flesh. Fresh pain, waves and waves of it, relentless.

I check my face in the mirror on the passenger's sun visor. I look pale. But he won't be able to see I've been crying. Brooke's makeup sorted that out.

The door opens, and I lean back over to my side. Harry gives me a curt nod as he climbs into the truck. He looks like he didn't get any sleep at all. Dark shadows under his eyes. And he hasn't shaven. His clothes are crumpled.

Oh.

I wait for him to say something, only he doesn't. The roof of my mouth feels like sandpaper against my tongue.

I should be friendly. I know that. It's not his fault he's not interested in me. Not his fault he wants a partner who is straight.

"Are you okay?" I ask him, trying to keep my voice light.

He nods. Doesn't say anything.

So, we drive around in silence. And the whole time, I try not to wonder if he really did sleep with Evie. And if so, why does he seem so down now?

At last, I switch the radio on, just to fill the awkwardness.

"*...is indeed correct and we can confirm that Charlie Less and Nikolai Ren are now in police custody. Neither Aleks Armstrong nor Julian Fennah were with Less and Ren, and the Met and Devon police are currently working on strategies to find the remaining two men. Experts from counter-terrorism forces across Europe are still being consulted. For the time-being, the county-wide lockdown for Devon will stay in place.*"

A box is waiting for me at the accommodation building when we get back. Grant calls me over as Harry and I enter the building. The box is huge. Amazon packaging. Oh, Harry's present. I frown, not sure it is a good idea to give it to him now. Then I stare at the box and frown harder. The box is way too big for a bow tie. Unless I've somehow ordered a gigantic one.

Harry disappears off to the men's toilets, still apparently sullen, so I take the penknife out of my pocket and cut through the tape on the box.

I open it.

And stare at the contents. Tiny alligators on bow ties.

So many of them.

"Oh my God," I say, running my hand through the contents of the box. A piece of paper snags against my fingers and I pull it out. Two bow ties fly out with it, and I hurriedly throw them back in the box. "One hundred?" I stare at the number on the packing slip.

I've ordered one-hundred?

My eyes drop to the bottom of the sheet of paper. Where the total price is. Dear Lord. I have spent eighty freaking pounds on bow ties. Eighty pounds! How didn't I notice when I paid?

I feel like screaming.

"All right?" Lisa asks as she saunters through the hallway, strapping a radio to her belt.

"Uh, yeah." I give her a smile, then fold the top of the box back down. Better move this to my room.

Brooke's going to have a field day when she finds out what I've done.

I lift the box up. It's not heavy, just an awkward shape, and I grimace. It's also right in front of my eyeline now and I can't see a thing. *Good one, Pols.*

"Hey, let me help you."

Of course it's Harry. His voice. And him. In front of the box, I think. The one person I now need to avoid.

Suddenly, his hands are against mine as he takes the box from me. I hate how his touch still sends electricity through me.

"What's in here?" he asks. "It's a lot lighter than I was expecting."

"Nothing."

"Nothing?" Unlike me, he holds the box lower, so he can still see where he's going and I can see his face. And, for the first time today, a small smile appears. I mean, he still looks awful, not himself at all, but there's a spark of *him* in his expression now. "You ordered a box of nothing?" He gives it a little shake.

"Sanitary towels," I say, because it's the first thing I can think of that he probably won't want to look at. And if he looks inside and sees the bow ties, he'll know why I ordered them. Well, maybe not why I ordered a hundred of them. But he'll *know*, I'm sure.

"A whole box of them?" He looks surprised.

"Five-year supply. Buying in bulk is cheaper."

Harry seems satisfied by that answer and doesn't say anything more. So neither do I—well, mainly because I don't know what to say and I just want this to be over with. I want to grab a coffee from the canteen before heading over to the petting farm center for my next shift. Luckily, although Evie runs that, the schedule has me and Brooke working together. Evie's doing the farm center accounts today. She's got Interstitial Cystitis and said she was in a lot of pain with that yesterday and needs to be as close to a toilet as possible today. From the look on Brooke's face when she heard that, she clearly thought that meant that Evie and Harry had slept together, as Evie's often told us that sex makes her IC flare up. But I don't want to believe that. And I know Evie—sort of. She told me once before that she wanted any sexual relations to be meaningful.

Just because Evie's got a flare-up of her condition, it doesn't mean anything happened between her and Harry. But it doesn't mean that they're not attracted to each other either, I remind myself.

"Well, thank you," I say to Harry as we reach my door. I take the box from him, then realize I haven't got a hand to actually open my door, even though the key's now in my fingers. But it's squashed against the box.

I put the box down awkwardly and fumble with the key.

"I would've carried it in for you," Harry says, his voice a little quiet again. His eyes lock onto mine, and there's something in them that I don't understand. Then the walls go up and the look disappears. He turns away. There's tension in his shoulders, and I want to reach out and massage the tension away.

But I can't.

"Thanks," I say.

Harry walks away, and I yank my door open and kick the box of bow ties over my threshold. Of course, the box catches on something, tips over, and a sea of bow ties spreads across my carpet. I groan and slam my door.

They're still on the floor when Brooke arrives to get changed into overalls ready for a pending shift. She tries not to laugh as she picks them up, and I try not to scream.

EIGHTEEN

Harry

"ALL RIGHT, MATE?" Morris asks as I join him in the stockroom. We're sorting feed out for the farm animals—not the ones in the petting farm, but the herd of dairy cattle. Friesians, I think they are.

Morris is a strange looking man, and it's the first time I've had a chance to talk with him. Before, I've only seen him in glimpses, lurking in the background. Now, I find he's got a really strong Australian accent.

"Spiffing," I say. And then what the hell? I've literally never said that word before.

"You don't look too happy," Morris says. "Report not going well?"

"Report?"

Morris laughs. "The reason you're here, the report about Goldwater."

Ah. I haven't even started it yet. And last night I had an email from my boss asking for an update. She's in London and of course she heard Devon is in lockdown. But she still said it's no excuse to have a holiday. I have work to do.

But I couldn't concentrate on it. Not when I knew Polly saw Evie flirting with me. And I guess she saw me flirting back. Because of course I did. I always do. It's like I can't help it.

Uni was the worst. So many girls flocking around me. Of course I slept with most of them. I almost couldn't help myself. Because when I was sleeping with a pretty girl who'd been making eyes at me across the club, I wasn't thinking about my dad's death. Sex was the only way I could stop the grief. And the sex was good and I felt amazing after, each time.

Bo persuaded me to see a therapist a couple years after Dad died. Because that's when all this—the sex—started. Martin, the therapist who always had a runny nose and the most horrendous blue denim jacket, said it was a coping method. Some people get more promiscuous when they're grieving.

It's a distraction method.

I didn't agree with him. I was in sixth form at the time. I mean, all my friends were sleeping with girls. And *they* weren't grieving. I was normal. But I was also the one with the reputation at parties. Not just in sixth form but at uni too.

And maybe I was performing. I mean, it felt good…and I was proud of my reputation, but it felt like it wasn't me. And whenever I thought about whether Dad would approve of my actions, I knew instantly that he wouldn't. He always said women are to be cherished. He and Mum married before they even slept together. Making love is sacred, he always said.

But I wasn't making love. I was just having sex. There's a difference.

And I liked the sex then.

Yet, last night, flirting with Evie was a challenge. One I set myself. Because if I'd been at school or uni then, I'd have slept with her no doubt. A brief distraction from my pain.

My guilt.

I swallow hard.

I didn't sleep with her last night. And I expected that my strength and willpower not to do it would make me feel better. Not like this.

But I saw the hurt in Polly's eyes, just like I saw it at that party when we were at school. She still likes me, and I still like her, and I'm still that guy who flirts with others in front of her. I groan. Now I've made her think I'm not interested in her. She's going to think it's because she's asexual, and that's why I chose Evie over her.

"Woah, not that one, mate," Morris says, and I realize I've got a scoop in my hand and have been shoveling grain into different buckets. I blink. "You look like you've had no sleep?"

"Just couldn't sleep."

"Oh?" Now he looks interested. "Worrying about anything in particular?"

I shake my head, but it's a lie. Polly and Brooke left the games room pretty soon after I was flirting with Evie. The look of hurt on Polly's face haunted me, and I left too, soon after that, with the aim of finding Polly. Even if Evie did try and persuade me to stay, by touching my arms a lot.

But I had to find Polly.

Only, I couldn't. She wasn't in her room—or if she was, she didn't answer. Wasn't in the canteen, nor any of the communal areas either.

She was avoiding me, hiding somewhere. And that's all I could focus on in the evening and night—so much so I forgot I'd been planning to do my laundry in the evening.

And then, this morning, I saw her. Same shift for patrol. And I should've said something, but I don't know what happened. I just clammed up. Couldn't think what to say, and I'm bad at apologies. And I was acutely aware of my rumpled clothes—having to re-wear ones I should've washed—and what it would look like to Polly. I thought about explaining the clothes situation, but then thought it could seem like I was explaining it too much, making it seem like I was lying.

So we drove around. In silence. And I tried to offer an olive branch by carrying that box upstairs, but she clearly didn't want to talk to me.

I really have blown it.

Morris natters away as we take the Land Rover over to the cattle barns. As we feed the animals, I keep a lookout for Polly, hoping to see her, even though she'll be at the petting farm now.

I don't.

"Don't look so glum, mate," Morris says. "Lockdown will be over soon. Then you can get back home. Now, in the meantime, you can help me look for Moggie. She missed her lunch earlier and that's not at all like her."

In the end, after my patrol shift and helping Brooke with animal records—a fun two hours in which Brooke glares at me and alternates between pursing her lips and sighing exasperatedly—I escape to my room. My boss's phone call has been weighing heavy over me. I need to start my report. I've noticed a lot of people do work—or maybe it's their own leisure—on laptops in the canteen. There's a plush sofa area to the far side where I've seen Lisa and Grant go a couple times with their own laptops or music players (Lisa uses earphones, Grant doesn't), but I need complete solitude to write this report. Or at least write something decent that maybe could be used.

I unlock my bedroom door and—

"What the hell?" I stare at the ginger cat on my bed, then my eyes widen as I see the kittens. "Oh my God."

NINETEEN

Polly

MOGGIE'S HAD KITTENS—great.

Not so great that she had them on Harry's bed. On top of a pile of crumpled washing.

Now, he's got to move out of that room—Lisa was very particular about that. You can't disturb a new mother.

Harry moving to the other spare room in the block—on the floor below, next to Evie's room—shouldn't make me sad. Not after it's been made clear he's not interested in me.

But it does make me sad.

And it's not like I can avoid him. Today's his birthday. That blasted box of bow ties sits next to my desk, taunting me, and all everyone's been talking about is the fancy-dress party tonight. Grant told me earlier that Harry's confident he'll win, but only Brooke and I know about my costume. And I try to use that to cheer me up.

But it doesn't.

I'm just in one of those bad moods that nothing can solve.

A bad mood that's made even worse when I realize I'm on patrol with Evie.

Wonderful.

Evie smiles warmly as we get into the patrol truck. "All right, Polly?"

Her eyes look even bigger today, make her look even more like a startled fawn. Her hair's tied back in a messy ponytail— the type that's actually time-consuming to create—but she's not got any makeup on now. I guess the last few days were just because Harry was new here.

And now she's not wearing makeup? Does that mean she's given up? Or she feels secure enough in her confidence that Harry likes her?

I frown. It shouldn't matter. Doesn't matter.

"That thing you did with the poachers the other day, that was amazing," Evie gushes. "No way I'd be brave enough to do that."

"Well," I say, trying to keep my voice light and friendly. "I didn't think he'd actually shoot."

"But he did."

Yes, I think, and then Harry saved me.

No, this truck is now a Harry-free zone. No thoughts on him.

"How's your sister and the baby?" I ask Evie. She's got an identical twin, and last I heard Ruby was recovering from a C-section.

"Yeah, they're doing good." Evie pulls out her phone. Her screensaver is a picture of a chubby baby. "Cute, right?"

I know all babies are supposed to be cute, but that is not a word I'd use for this baby. He's staring straight at the camera, a stern look on his face. There are lines around his mouth that just add to his strange expression. And he's got a full head of hair. It's blond, I think, but the lighting makes some parts of it look grey.

I nod. "Very cute."

She laughs. "Well, now you're being polite. Because that baby looks like an old man. See his expression?"

I give a tentative smile.

"Everyone says it. Even Rubes." She puts her phone away. "Which route is it this morning?"

"Down by the lake," I say.

We set off. She drives. I'm in the passenger seat.

"Looking forward to the party tonight?" she asks me after a few moments.

"Yeah," I say. Even if I'm not. Not when she's going to be there, fawning all over Harry.

I want to dislike Evie, my rival, but I can't. She is nice. It's not her fault that Harry's interested in her and not me.

"What's your costume like?" Evie asks. "I've got this one of Wonder Woman." She glances at me, through her thick lashes. "It sounds a little slutty, but it's actually not. All this—" she indicates her cleavage, "—is completely covered up. Ah, not that I should use the word *slutty*." Her gaze becomes troubled, then she says, "So what is your costume like? Did you buy one especially?"

I shake my head. "Nope. Had it a while. But it's a surprise."

"A surprise." Evie's eyes light up and she seems genuinely excited. "Ooooh. How exciting. Now, you'd only say that if you're planning on winning."

TWENTY

Harry

POLLY LETS ME *in the backdoor. "We're going to have to be quiet,"
she says. In the background, I can hear her parents arguing. Then the
sound of her brother's voice is there as well. The three of them are yelling
as Polly leads me up to her room.*

*The history project's already spread out on her bed, and she sits at her
desk, facing me.*

*I guess that leaves the bed for me to sit on. I try not to disturb the
papers.*

*Polly starts talking about the work that needs doing next on the
project, but it's hard to concentrate, what with her parents and brother
yelling, and the fact that I'm in Polly Brady's room.*

*It's a cute room. Small, minimal furnishings, but what furnishings
there are have been carefully chosen. It's all color-coordinated. Golds and
reds. There's a poster of an African elephant on the wall, and her
lampshade has elephants on it too. Elephants. She must like them.*

I make a mental note.

"What do you think?" Polly asks.

"Uh, yeah," I say.

She points to the textbook next to me. "Think it's on page forty."

I turn to page forty, forcing myself to get back into study mode.

We work for a few hours, and then Polly says, "I think that's everything?" She looks at me, like she's uncertain.

"We've finished already?" I frown. "This was supposed to take all term."

She runs through the checklist quickly before looking back at me. "Yep, we've definitely done everything."

"So what do we do now?" I ask. Downstairs, it's now quiet. There was a lot of slamming of doors earlier, and then nothing.

"Want to watch something?" she asks.

"Sure." I route around in my bag and produce my DVD of Jaws. *I put it in my rucksack this morning, meaning to let Brad borrow it as I still can't believe he's not seen it, but then he disappeared off with Brooke before I could give it to him. "I've got this with me."*

Polly laughs but grabs her laptop and loads the DVD into it. Then she moves to her bed, sits sort of next to me.

As the film starts, I want to reach across, put my arms around her. But I don't.

I don't think she feels the same way.

So, we just watch the film. And the whole time I imagine what it would be like to kiss her.

TWENTY-ONE

Polly

"YOU SURE YOU'RE not going to be too hot?" Brooke sounds worried. And she'd look worried too—if I could see her.

"Argh," I mumble, my balance going. I fall to the right, stumble against my bed. This blasted T-rex costume is smaller than I remember.

"You're about halfway," Brooke says. "What is the inner bit made of, Lycra?"

I grumble something, and then feel her hands as she tries to tug it down my body. There are two layers to the costume— there's an inner skin-tight suit that supposedly stretches and molds around you, but feels like it's suffocating me, and then there's the outer T-rex-shaped costume that needs inflating once I've got the Lycra part on.

"Stop! It's got my bra!" I yell into the hot fabric and have my breath fog back over me like a thick blanket.

Brooke and I do a lot of shimmying and contorting in order to rescue my breasts from their new-found prison. The adjustment isn't that much of an improvement, really, not for my sore breasts. I remember this costume being a lot roomier when I first tried it on.

"I don't think this is a unisex costume," Brooke says when we've finally lined up the eye-holes of the skin-tight inner layer with my eyes (and the eye-holes in the outer part of the garment) so I can see. She gestures down toward my crotch. "It's, uh, kind of baggy here. Lots of room. Unlike up here, where your boobs are."

"Wonderful," I mutter. "It'll be okay once the dinosaur part is inflated. Have you got the pump?"

Brooke retrieves it and then attaches it to the tail of the costume. The hand-pump squeaks with every squeeze. And it takes a *long* time to inflate the whole thing.

I can't wait for this party to be over. Why did I ever think wearing this costume would be a good idea? Especially when Harry doesn't like me. It'll just make me stand out like a sore thumb. And make me look strange, wearing an ill-fitting man's dinosaur costume. And, I mean, it should be impossible for a dinosaur costume to even be ill-fitting—because who doesn't fit in a freaking dinosaur costume?

I've got half a mind to beg Brooke to help me get this thing off, but then someone's banging on our door.

Brooke lets Grant in, who does a double take when he sees me.

"Wow," he says. He's dressed as Iron Man. "Just...wow." He's laughing.

I am not laughing. I am regretting my costume choice already.

"You got the playlist?" he asks Brooke, who nods and waves her iPhone at him.

"You made a playlist?" I ask Brooke, but the costume muffles my voice and doesn't sound at all like me.

"Grant asked me to," Brooke says, her tone even.

"I can't believe you three went to school together," Grant says. He tips his head to the side, and the angle makes him look more like Lisa, his sister. "Small world, huh?"

The three of us out head out of the room and down to the canteen. The tables and chairs have been stacked against the wall, leaving a huge space free. The space for the party.

"Get the music started, Brooke," Lisa says. She has a horse mask pushed up so it sits on the top of her head and a red tinsel tail attached to her waistband. She turns and looks at my costume. "Nice."

Brooke heads over to where Evie is setting up speakers. Her Wonder Woman costume is indeed pretty modest. Next to her, Morris and Jane are sorting out a drinks table, which mainly consists of one large bowl of what I assume to be fruit punch.

"Presents, we haven't got any presents!" Evie shouts suddenly. "Shoot, he's going to be here soon."

There's a moment where everyone looks at each other with blank faces.

"Uh, I've got enough for all of us," I say, thinking of the bow ties. I weigh up my options. On the one hand, it would be hilarious if we all gave the same thing. But, on the other hand, isn't that a ridiculous idea? Us all giving the same thing? And then it wouldn't be a special thing that I give him...

"You have?" Morris blinks at me.

"What about wrapping paper?" Jane asks. "It's a birthday. You can't give presents unwrapped."

"There's tissue paper in the gift shop," Evie says. "I don't think there's much though. It's only for the ornaments."

"Get it," Jane says, just as Lisa says, "He doesn't need presents wrapped."

"We should wrap some," Evie says.

That seems to be the compromise, because then Grant and I are heading back up to my room to get the box.

He frowns a little as he picks out one bow tie. The cartoon crocodiles on it are all pulling different expressions. "These are nice and all, but why buy a hundred?"

"Mistake," I mutter, breathing hard. Wow, this suit is hot. My skin's sticking to the material, and I'm already melting.

Grant heaves the box up—putting too much effort in, probably thinking it's heavier than it is, and the box flies up. He just about manages to stop the bow ties flying everywhere.

By the time we get back to the canteen, we've got five minutes until Harry's supposed to be here. On the way down the stairs, Grant told me he's got Harry doing a timed test. Something to make him an 'official ranger.' Harry fell for it of course. Apparently, he seemed eager.

"That's a lot of bow ties," Evie says, peering into the box. She speaks loudly because Brooke's playlist is now playing— and it's all the songs from Harry and Brad's favorite bands when we were at school.

Brooke just snorts. She's already laughed her head off many a time about my mistake.

"Okay, just wrap a few," Jane says. "We can use the rest for decoration."

"If that's okay with Polly?" Grant looks at me. "They are hers."

I nod. The protruding jaw of the dinosaur hits my chest.

There's no way I can wrap the bow ties, or even artfully place them around the canteen, not with the inflatable hands of my costume. So, I sort of end up watching everyone.

Watching as Jane ladles out the punch into plastic cups and hands them around. I can't take hold of mine so it goes onto the table next to me.

Watching as Evie starts talking to Grant, causing Brooke to quickly step closer to Grant. Hmm. Interesting. Brooke and Grant? My eyes narrow as I watch them. She's mirroring his body language. He keeps glancing at her, a tender look on his face. And Brooke's completely turning her back on Evie, forcing her out of the conversation—even though Evie was only talking. Definitely not flirting.

But Brooke and Grant? He's like *forty*.

He's—

And that's when I see Harry.

"Surprise!" everyone yells. Except me, because I've frozen. And why are they even shouting surprise? Harry knows about this party. We discussed it in front of him.

In front of Harry.

Harry.

Oh my God.

His costume.

Harry sees me, and his mouth drops open.

Harry and I have the same costume. Just in different colors. Mine is green, his is a dark red.

"Did you two plan this?" Morris shouts, from where he's slouched in a chair, nursing a drink.

"No," I say, feeling heat rush to my face. Embarrassment. Why am I even being flooded with embarrassment? It was my decision to wear this.

"Oh my God, are those crocodile bow ties?" Harry's eyes are wide, and matching costumes apparently forgotten, he grabs a bow tie (with some difficulty, due to his dinosaur hands) from one of the tables at the side of the room.

"It *is* a crocodile bow tie," Evie purrs, gravitating toward him.

Harry's gaze springs to her, like she's a magnet.

"Polly got them all," Brooke shouts from the other side of the room.

Harry looks toward me, and his eyes meet mine. Surprise is clear on his face, and something more. Something deeper? And I want to say it's a really meaningful moment, but of course we're both dressed as dinosaurs and he can't even see my face. Maybe I should follow suit and take the headpiece off.

"Come on, we've got games planned," Lisa says. She points to where the chairs are stacked at the side. "Let's do musical chairs."

"Musical chairs?" Harry looks even more surprised.

"Lisa loves kids' games," I say, but the costume distorts my voice, and I'm not even sure he hears it.

"Well, we're not going to be quick enough to win musical chairs," Harry says, indicating himself and me.

I waddle over to where Lisa's now organizing the chairs. My tail seems heavier, swings from side to side.

"Then we can have the food," Grant says. "After the games. Oh, where's the food?"

"Thought you were doing the food?" Jane says.

Grant looks to George. "I thought it was you?"

Brooke snorts. Lisa looks unimpressed.

"It's fine," Harry says. "We don't need food. Come on, let's play musical chairs."

Playing musical chairs to some old track by Eminem is weird. So weird. But everyone's laughing. And, predictably, Harry and I are the first ones out of the game. We're not exactly nimble.

"Want a drink?" Harry asks.

"Sure," I say. Though shouldn't it be me offering him one? Given it's his birthday and all.

We head over to the table. As well as the bowl of punch, there are now a few cans. Harry tries to pick one up with his clawed inflatable hand. Then he pulls the gloves off and pushes down the head-piece so the T-rex's jaws are sticking weirdly out behind his head. He peels the skin-tight Lycra face piece down.

I do the same, with the head and the hands of my costume. Cold air rushes against me. Oh my god. I can *breathe* again.

"Looks like we're both going to win best costume," I say to Harry after he hands me a cup of fruit punch. Because I can't think of what to say and this is awkward, standing with him by the wall, watching the others play musical chairs. Twice, Evie nearly ends up sitting in Grant's lap.

"I guess we will," Harry says, taking another swig of his drink. His throat makes a small gulping sound as he swallows it. "You remembered about the bow tie with crocodiles on it."

"Of course," I say, because I remember everything he's ever said to me.

"I can't believe it." He smiles as he grabs the nearest bow tie. "It looks exactly like that one I wished I'd got."

"I know."

"And you bought fifty?"

"A hundred," I say. "Though that was by accident. I thought I was just ordering one."

He grins, shakes his head a little in slow motion as he does it. "You should return them."

"Yeah," I say. But they've all been removed from their protective plastic bags now. "But now you'd never need to pop one in the laundry. Just wear a clean one each day."

Eminem stops, and there's a flurry of movement as everyone else still playing scrabbles for a chair.

"What's next, pass the parcel?" Harry laughs.

"Knowing Lisa, probably," I say. "Or rounders. She likes rounders."

"In here?"

"No. Outside. It's always the same prize for whoever wins rounders—she changes the rules a bit, so it'll be pairs playing rather than teams. But she has these huge plastic bees. They're flasks, but they look hideous. The winning pairs get to keep the bees for a week before returning them to her vault."

Harry's eyes sparkle. "Wow, a whole week. We better win them then."

"We?"

"Well, we've won the fancy dress," he says. "We have to have won that. I wonder what our prize will be for that... And we make a good team, good track record of winning—remember that final history project? So why jinx things by partnering with others?"

My gaze finds Evie. She's the most competitive player of musical chairs that I know. And sure, she's certainly playing as competitively as usual, but I can't help but notice she's grimacing a lot like she's in pain.

"Okay," I say.

"If...if that's okay?" Harry asks.

I nod. "Yeah, of course. Oh, happy birthday, by the way," I add, realizing I haven't said it yet. I didn't see Harry earlier. We were on different shifts and I had a quick breakfast in my room rather than the canteen. And then Evie and I were out on the long patrol to the lake, and we took lunch with us. That journey takes hours.

"Thank you." Harry smiles. Then he turns more toward me, so he's staring right at me.

"Okay, right. Well," he says, and he sounds nervous. "This is either going to go really well or really badly." He goes to run a hand through his hair, then stops. I realize his hair's gelled slightly for the occasion. Oh, it's gelled into scales? Quite bad scales, but scales nonetheless. "I like you, Polly. I always have done. At school. And I wish I'd been brave enough before to tell you. But it hasn't changed, and seeing you these last few days... and I... I think you like me?"

He likes me? I stare at him. My heart thumps like crazy. A strange fizzing sensation fills me. Harry Weller likes me? He always has done.

The music stops. Suddenly the silence seems deafening.

"Okay, I think that's Jane out," Lisa says, and Jane's huffing loudly, and then Eminem blares out again.

And I'm still staring at Harry. At the warmth in his eyes. And I realize he's waiting for me to answer, so I nod, don't trust myself to speak, because knowing me my voice will suddenly be all squeaky and I'll sound like I've inhaled helium.

Relief floods Harry's face. He reaches out and touches my arm. Or at least the inflatable dinosaur arm. He steps closer still, and I'm stepping closer to him, and Eminem blares out again.

Harry leans toward me, and my heart pounds.

He's going to kiss me. He's actually going to kiss me and—

"But I'm ace," I blurt out. And what the hell? He knows this. Why am I making it sound like some big, unexpected reveal? And like it's a problem.

It is a problem. You're not compatible.

But Fran and Ivan are and—

"So you don't want to kiss?" Harry frowns. "I thought you said—"

"I did say. I do." Suddenly, it feels a million degrees here. "Kissing's fine. But I'm not having sex." And I don't want him to think that just because it's his birthday that I will. Even though I don't think he'd think that. Harry's not like that.

"Not everything's about sex, Polly." He sounds amused.

"But I'm sex-repulsed—you asked me before and Brooke cut in before I could answer. But it's important you know and…"

"It's fine," he says. "Really. It's you I like."

"Even though I likely won't ever want to have sex?" I lower my voice. "I don't want you thinking that somehow I'll want to later—like, it's not a reflection on you if I don't, and well, I probably won't. It's part of me—I just… I've never felt sexual attraction and I haven't wanted to do it, and the time when I did, it just really affected me…" I don't even know how to say it. "Sex just made me want to avoid the person completely, never see them again because I felt nauseous just thinking about them, let alone seeing them."

His eyes seem to swallow me up. "I understand. Polly, you haven't hidden this from me, Polly. I understand. It's *you* I want. It's you I've always wanted."

"But what about…your needs?"

He laughs. "I can take care of that. Believe me, I've done a lot of research on this. There are forums about making ace/allo relationships work."

Relationships. He really is thinking about a *relationship* with me.

"Now, is it okay if I kiss you?" he asks.

I feel myself blushing. "Yes."

Harry smiles then leans in to kiss me.

This time, I don't stop him.

TWENTY-TWO

Polly

WELL, I MAY not stop him from kissing me, but our dinosaur costumes do. We physically cannot get close enough due to the inflatable outfits and the ways the T-rexes' jaws have each somehow swung around and are bashing into each other like balloons.

Harry and I burst out laughing.

He takes my hand instead. His touch is warm and safe and it's not quite like an electric touch, like it has been before, because it feels stronger now. Like he's grounding me.

"And the winner is Evie!" Lisa shouts, and there's a round of applause, and Evie looks over and sees me and Harry, so close together.

Sadness fills her eyes for a moment, then she blinks it away and smiles at us, before she heads quickly to the bathroom. I feel a little bad, but then Harry's pulling me closer again—as close as the costumes will allow.

"Time for rounders!" Lisa shouts.

Everyone cheers. Even me and Harry.

"Later," he says, his eyes twinkling. "We'll have that kiss later."

We win the plastic bees, me and Harry. Well, we win them for a week. But I can't stop smiling as we head down to the games room—because that's apparently where everyone is going after the party.

Harry leads me to the sofas, to the one where Brooke and I sat last time. And Brooke, she's here too. I can tell she's keeping an eye on me and Harry.

I turn my back to her and face Harry. He reaches out for my arms. We've both taken the dinosaur costumes off now. Had to, given the game of rounders. Mine's safely back in my wardrobe. I feel a bit weird that it's my brother's costume as it's what is bringing me and Harry together.

Harry stares into my eyes. He's good at making direct eye contact. What seems like an eternity passes, and he doesn't look away. It's making me dizzy, and it feels so intimate. I wonder if this is the moment that will lead to our first kiss, but wondering that only makes me laugh. I always laugh when I'm nervous.

He smiles. I look down. On the sofa between us are the two plastic bees. Really, they're hideous. The green one has a massive dent in it and the yellow one's got a lot of scratches on it.

"So, which uni did you go to?" Harry asks.

The question seems so awkward—like neither of us actually knows what to do next—that I nearly laugh. "Reading. Studied Ecology and Wildlife Conservation," I say. "Same as Brooke."

"You two always did do practically everything together at school," he says with a laugh. "Remember when we got paired up for that first history project together, and Brooke was fuming?"

I laugh. "Yeah, she spoke to Ms. Lake about it." Then I turn quickly, remembering Brooke's in hearing distance. I hope she doesn't think I'm laughing at her. But she's got earphones in now, probably listening to the latest report on the lockdown and the remaining two terrorists. I turn back to Harry. "So, what did you do? Journalism, if you're a reporter?"

Harry nods. "At London South Bank. Various internships there afterward, but the last one was with *Word Zero*, and then they took me on as a junior reporter. I was surprised to get this gig though, the Goldwater one—they normally only send their senior reporters out to places like this. Before this, I was just covering local things. Spending so much time on the Tube. Most of the time was spent just traveling around, getting annoyed at how busy it is. Because it's ridiculously busy, and I still can't get used to London."

"What's it like?" I ask. "Being a journalist? Stressful?"

"Can be," he says, his voice soft. "Well, it is. I've realized that since coming here, and I've only been here a few days. But just the atmosphere at Goldwater, it's so different. So much more relaxed. In London, it's a constant go-go-go with no breaks. Everyone's busy, but it kind of feels like you don't actually know anyone, just because everyone's so busy. Or you only see the part of the person they want you to see. Whereas here, it's more...whole."

"Whole?"

"Organic," he says.

I've leant in toward him as he was speaking, without even realizing I was doing it. And he's done the same, a mirror to my actions. Only six inches—and falling—between our faces.

"Here, I feel like I know people. Know you," he says. His eyes are dark pools that nearly swallow me up. "Though I knew you anyway, Polly. I just… I feel like I know you better now than even when we were at school."

I can hardly breathe. Three inches between us. We're going to kiss. We're going to kiss! The teenager in me can hardly contain her excitement.

"Yeah," Harry says, placing his hand on mine. With his other hand, he removes the plastic bees from the space between us. "You've always been this incredible light, Polly. Always. But now you're just even brighter. And everything around you seems dim in comparison, because it's like you're the sun. And I feel like I'm home… Well." He laughs under his breath. "The sun would burn me to smithereens if it was literally my home." His eyes do that shifty thing that he used to do sometimes when we were working on our history projects. "You know what I mean," he says.

I nod. "I do."

The space between us disappears as his lips brush mine.

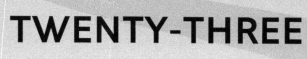

TWENTY-THREE

Harry

EVERYONE'S LEFT THE games room, apart from me and Polly. The clock just struck midnight, and it feels intimate, here, with her. Polly's lying against me on the sofa, and my arms are around her. And it feels right. It feels like coming home.

Like I've found her, finally. I'm with her, and this was always meant to be.

Polly yawns.

"Tired?" I ask her.

She nods, still managing to look incredibly cute. "And I'm on an early shift tomorrow."

"Earlier than seven?"

She nods. "Six. Helping Morris with the milking." She wrinkles her nose. "Hate doing that."

"Well, you better get some sleep then," I say, and I want to invite her to stay in my room. My new room—where there isn't a cat and kittens—has a double bed. But I don't want to seem too forward. I don't want to make Polly think that this is about hooking up, when it isn't.

I want to fall asleep with her in my arms. Because now I've found her and I'm holding her, I don't want to let go of her. I want to be with her always.

"Okay," she says, sleepily.

We kiss goodnight—several times—then I walk her to her room, give her another kiss. I'm smiling as she shuts the door. And I can't believe it—Polly and me. And it feels so right, and we're going to make this work.

We will. We were always meant to be together.

———————

The next morning I've got three hours off to start writing my report. Lisa said she'd only schedule me for afternoons for some days, so as to give me time to do the job I was actually sent here for.

I grab a quick breakfast in the canteen—it's seven o'clock, and Polly will already be at the farm—and I swear there's a bounce to my step as I grab a toasted teacake and head to a nearby table.

"Hey, Harry."

I turn at the voice. Evie. Immediately, I feel on guard.

"Um, I just wanted to ask. You and Polly... It's serious, isn't it?"

I nod. "I hope so."

She smiles weakly, and I can see she's trying to cover up her disappointment. "Cool. Well, I'll see you around then. And don't worry, I won't flirt anymore. Or, at least, I'll try not to."

Evie leaves, and my teacake's gone cold. I chew it methodically. Then I think about Polly again, and my mood lightens. I pull out my phone and I'm about to text Sara to tell her about me and Polly, when I stop. My last message to her—one asking about Mum—has gone unanswered.

I flick to the conversation stream with Bo. That one's the same.

I frown. Maybe it's the signal here.

I mean, if there was anything wrong, they'd let me know.

I meet Polly at the barn as she finishes her shift a few hours later. It's nearly ten, though it feels much later, and I wrap her in a hug.

"Ugh, I'm all sweaty," she says. "And smelly. Let me shower first."

"I don't mind," I say, nuzzling her neck. And it feels good to be this close to her finally—just like how I imagined we'd be when we were eighteen.

I take her hand, and she squeezes it. I like the way it feels, our fingers interlaced. She looks up at me and smiles. There's energy in her eyes that just seems to wrap around me, ground me. Energy that makes me feel this is right. More right than it's ever been.

"Do you remember Ice Cream Day?" I ask her.

Polly nods, smiling. "Of course."

"We should do that again," I say. "Just the two of us though. You have ice cream here, right?"

"Be some in the kitchen," she says.

"It's a date then," I say.

Polly laughs. So do I. And we're still laughing and giggling when we get into the accommodation block.

"Why don't we get the ice cream now?" she says.

"Now?"

"Yeah, I'm not working again until after lunch. We could be rebels and have dessert before the main course."

I can't help but grin. And I got plenty of reporting work done this morning—drafting out a first draft of the gala report and info on Goldwater—so I can spare the time.

"Deal," I say.

"I'll just shower first," she says. "Meet you in the canteen in fifteen."

I've never known a woman to take just fifteen minutes showering, but Polly does. She's even washed her hair and toweled it dry. It hangs damp and wavy around her shoulders, and it's made wet patches on her shirt.

"Find any ice cream?" she asks.

I shake my head. "Though I didn't really look." I mean, I've only got food before from the canteen when it's been on the serving hatches—George is the cook—and it felt intrusive to actually go into the kitchen area.

Polly, however, has no such reservations and acts like she's done it hundreds of times before as she leads me around, behind the serving counters and into a sectioned-off room. There's a large chest-freezer against the wall, which she opens.

"Can you hold the lid?" she asks. "It's heavy."

I hold it up as she rummages through the contents of the freezer. The freezer itself is divided into three columns. Frozen meat is in the first, frozen veg and what looks like pastry in the second, and the third has deserts.

"Found some!" Polly says, pulling out a small tub. "You still like mint choc chip, right?"

"Of course."

We leave the kitchen and move to sit down at one of the tables, but Polly stops me. "Let's sit in my room," she says. "It's cooler there. Canteen gets really hot."

For some reason, as I follow Polly to her room, I start to get nervous. And I don't understand it. This is Polly. But I'm worried I'm going to embarrass myself. Like I'll see her bed and imagine sex with her—even though I know it won't happen—but that, somehow, she'll know what I'm thinking about.

"You okay?" Polly asks.

I nod, and we reach her room. She unlocks it swiftly.

"Don't trip on the threshold," she says. "They all stick up."

In her room, we sit on her bed and eat our ice cream. She has some plastic cutlery in one of her drawers that we use. And it is good ice cream—I've never remembered ice cream on Ice Cream Day tasting this good.

After we've finished eating, Polly moves closer to me, so we're sitting right next to each other, our thighs touching. I reach out and place my hand on her leg. She smiles.

And we kiss.

TWENTY-FOUR

Polly

KISSING HARRY IS everything I imagined it would be. His lips are firm and soft and he gives short kisses that then begin to get deeper and longer.

My arms wrap around him and his around me, and we're holding each other tightly.

And this is perfect.

Our kisses deepen still, and then we're lying back on the bed, each on our sides, facing each other. My eyes close as he comes in for another kiss, and this feels right...

It feels nothing like lying with Peter.

Peter.

I jolt.

"Are you okay?" Harry asks.

I nod, pushing all thoughts of Peter aside. This is just me and Harry, and I was a fool before to think that the only person who'd want to be with me was Peter. Because Harry wants to be with me. And he's okay with me being asexual, and he's accepted every part of me.

TWENTY-FIVE
Polly

"LOOK, POLLY, THIS *isn't really fair,*" Peter says. *We're lying on my bed.* "*You're turning me on, and I... I've got needs.*"

I roll onto my side to face him. "*Then go and sort yourself out.*" *I flick my gaze toward the bathroom. The door's just behind him.*

But Peter doesn't move.

"*I don't know how you can really think this can work,*" *he says.* "*Like, I'm a reasonable guy. I'm not going to make you do anything. But relationships are about compromise. I'm giving up sex for you, but you're... you're not having to make any compromises. I don't want to use the word selfish, but it just seems like I'm the only one making these compromises, and you're just expecting me to do whatever you want.*"

I sit up. My shoulders tighten, and I can't help but feel hurt.

"*And I've read on those forums about how aces will have sex to please their partners. Don't you want to please me?*"

A cold shiver runs through my body. Emotional blackmail. I didn't think he'd stoop so low.

"*You do love me, don't you?*" *Peter says.*

And I nod, though I can't say the words out loud—because what I feel for Peter now is different than anything I'd felt for Harry. But what I felt for Harry wasn't real. And what I feel for Peter is. And Peter's here. Harry's not.

And I do like Peter.

Or at least, I did before this conversation.

"Aren't you even interested to know what it feels like? I mean, how can you know you're sex-repulsed if you've never done it?"

"I've never murdered someone, but I know I don't want to do that," I say drily.

"That's different," he says. "That's a question of morals. Having sex isn't." He shakes his head. "I just don't see how you can know you're truly ace if you won't even try it with me."

"I don't want to try it though," I say. "I don't experience sexual attraction. And I have no desire to do anything sexual... And the thought of it..." I cut myself off before I can offend him. "Look, you're heterosexual. I'm not. You wouldn't be asking a lesbian to have sex with you, knowing she's not sexually attracted to you. You'd accept her sexuality. And, right now, it feels like you're not accepting mine."

Peter sighs for a long time, then nods. "Okay, sorry." He grimaces for a moment. "It's just all new to me. I'll get used to it, I will."

"Seriously?" Brooke stares at me. "He said that to you?" Only she actually uses way more colorful language.

I nod. Tears are still running down my face, and I feel stupid about crying. But maybe Peter is right.

"You should just break up with him," she says, drawing me in for a hug. "Look, it's been a few months, and he's being like this? Pols, it's just going to get worse. I... I don't think you two are compatible."

"No, it's just me being silly."

Brooke shakes her head. *"It's not just you being silly. It's him being a colossal…"*

I miss her last word because I blow my nose loudly.

"Man, I'm going to kill him," she mutters. *"I never liked him."*

That just makes me cry harder.

"Look, there's the LGBT+ society. I'm sure there's got to be an ace guy there that you can meet."

"Doesn't mean there'd be any chemistry," I say.

"But you don't want to have sex anyway." She frowns.

"But there needs to be emotional chemistry. Physical attraction. Kinds like that." I shake my head. Brooke doesn't get it. *"I do have those with Peter."*

"Really?" She raises his eyebrows. *"Because he's had you crying for the last hour, or however long you've been here before I got back. That doesn't sound like an emotional or physical connection. Or any other good kind."*

"Peter's right, though," I say. *"Being ace is selfish."*

Brooke snorts. *"No, that's* him *being selfish and thinking about his needs only. Not thinking about the consequences this is having on you. He's trying to coerce you."*

"He's not!"

"Why else would he bring all that up when you've already made it perfectly clear what's acceptable and what's not?"

I haven't got an answer, so I just cry some more.

"Pols, you have to break up."

"I don't want to. He's the only guy who's ever been interested in me."

"But this isn't right. He's trying to coerce you into having sex. And I'm worried he's going to succeed."

TWENTY-SIX

Polly

THE TV BLARES out sound, all tinny and stutters.

"*In accordance with… Yes, counter-terrorism recommendations and latest intel… and the location of Aleks Armstrong and Julian Fennah… That's right, the county-wide lockdown of Devon is now being reduced to…*" the reporter on TV says. She's standing in a deserted street of Torquay. Seagulls flock around her.

"To where?" Brooke asks. "Did anyone catch that?"

I lean forward toward the TV. As does everyone else in the canteen. The TV's tiny and mounted on the wall by the door.

A pop-up map fills the TV screen, and the reporter speaks over it as the red mark that was filling the county reduce in size. "*As you can see, it is now only this region down here in the south of Devon that will remain in lockdown.*"

There are groans all around as the map shows that anything south of Ivybridge, South Brent, Totnes, and Paignton are still in lockdown. Typical—the one part of Devon that's still in lockdown, and we're right in the middle of it.

"Well, at least we're not the only nature reserve still in lockdown," Lisa says.

Slapton Ley Field Centre is too. They're by far the better facility for research and education. They've got links with many universities, whereas we're more linked to the local Primary and Secondary schools and clubs for our educational facilities.

I stir my soup. I already ate way too much ice cream and I'm not hungry at all now.

"What if they actually *do* turn up at Goldwater?" Evie asks, her voice sticky, like bubble-gum. "I mean, it'd be just our luck."

"Then we call the police," Lisa says. "Don't approach anyone dangerous." Her eyes flick to me, then she stands up. "Right. Back to work everyone."

Grant and I drive over to the northern border of Goldwater to finish the maintenance work that we started before. It's a rough drive, especially the last mile or so which has no track. We just drive over rough terrain.

"So, you and Harry Weller," Grant says with a mischievous look. "I was sure it was going to be Evie he went with."

"Me too." I try to keep my voice light, but worry seeps in. What if Harry can't go without sex and he goes to Evie, knowing she's straight? I know others online who are ace and have open relationships, so their partners can have their needs met, and it works for them but I know how much that would destroy me. I'm firmly monogamous. I don't want to share Harry, don't want to think about him with another woman.

Even if I can't give him what I need.

Peter called me selfish for these views. I cried when he said that, and Brooke had a go at him about it when she next saw him. It didn't stop me feeling selfish though, and now all these worries are transferring to Harry.

Stop. I try to breathe evenly. Harry hasn't actually said anything.

Grant and I reach the border fence and hop out. In the back of the truck, we've got a pole-driver, reels of wire fencing, and wooden posts. We're repairing a bit of the old fence. Not my favorite job.

Grant starts by slamming one of the poles against the ground, pointy-end first, right by the existing fence, until it's made a little divot. Then I haul over the new fence post and position it into place. Grant carries the pole-driver, grimacing under its weight, and I take one of its handles. We brace ourselves as we lift it up, to head-height, so we can place it over the post. Then we stand either side of the post, each holding with two hands onto a handle of the rusty pole-driver.

"Ready?" Grant asks.

"Yes."

It's hard work, lifting the pole-driver up and slamming it down, but each slamming forces the wooden post into the earth. Each slamming also makes me sweat loads—and I'm talking sweating buckets.

By the time we've got the post in a good foot and a half, I'm hot and sticky and Grant's face is bright red.

"Just six more to go," he says, his voice anything but cheerful.

No one likes putting up the new fencing.

Harry greets me with a kiss when I get back. I shower and then we grab food quickly, then he asks if I want to go to his room. Just to watch a DVD on his laptop.

"Be nice, just the two of us," he says.

Nerves fill me as I follow him, and I try to calm myself. Try not to think about what Peter said. And why the hell am I thinking about that now?

I haven't ever been in Harry's new room before—even before he occupied it. It's usually reserved for the day-time staff to go to hang out in their breaks or rest or shower or whatever. And it's a lot smaller than the room Brooke and I share.

Though it has got a double bed. And I can't stop staring at it.

"Do you want to sit?" Harry asks me, gesturing at the bed.

I nod, sit down. He sits next to me. And it feels…strange. I don't know. I'm too hyperaware of everything now.

"So, how's your family?" Harry asks. "You've not spoken about them, I don't think?"

My family.

I swallow hard, feel sick. The nausea's there instantly. It always is when anyone asks an innocent question.

"They died," I say. "Car accident. A few years ago."

I can't say anything more. It's like my throat's closing, literally stopping the words from coming out. Keeping them inside me, so I can't face the reality of their deaths any more than I already have.

"Oh, God, Polly. I'm so sorry."

The light in Harry's eyes darkens. "I had no idea." He looks genuinely upset.

"It's fine," I say. But how can the deaths of my family ever be fine?

I look around for something to change the conversation to and spot a vase of flowers on the window sill. "So you like roses?" I ask, indicating them. They're bright pink.

"No, they were already in here," he says. "Though I did change their water. It was really slimy and green. Didn't smell great."

I manage a small smile.

"Shall we watch the film now?" he asks. "You can choose what it is."

He grabs a tote bag from the foot of the bed and hands it to me. Inside, there are ten DVDs.

"You brought these with you?"

"Well, on the phone Lisa said internet wasn't great and I didn't want to be bored if Netflix wouldn't work."

I select a DVD at random. *Jaws*.

"Very romantic," Harry says with a smile.

He produces a laptop and slides the DVD in. A minute or so later, *Jaws* is on and the laptop's on the dresser opposite us. I shift a bit on the bed to get comfy, and Harry slides his arm around me.

By about ten minutes later, we end up leaning back, against the headboard, sort of half lying. And it feels nice lying down with him. And this is Harry Weller. Still, a part of me can't believe it. And I'm so aware of him—of his every move, how his arm's around me, and the rise and fall of his chest, and the sound of his breathing—I can barely concentrate on the film.

I tell myself just to relax. And it's silly, I was relaxed before with him. It's just because I ended up thinking about Peter. About how he said I was selfish.

And Harry's going to think the same thing.

He nestles closer to me, and I can smell his aftershave. I try to relax against him, but I'm too inside my head now. So I force myself to try and concentrate on *Jaws*, which only means I'm concentrating so hard that I can't actually pay attention to it—not that I need to, I know what happens because we watched it before, all those years ago—but the whole being unable to concentrate thing irritates me and almost makes the situation worse.

Not to mention I'm sweating. Not quite as much as earlier, doing the fencing with Grant, but enough that I'm now super self-conscious of that too. Silently, I curse my nerves. I always sweat when I'm worried.

And I shouldn't be worried!

I shake my head hard, as if I can shake out the worries.

"Are you okay?" Harry looks alarmed.

I jolt a little, part of me unaware that I literally shook my head. Like it believed I was only shaking my mind. I let out a small laugh. "Fine."

"Polly? *Are* you okay?"

"Yeah." My voice is too high.

Harry pauses the film. "What's wrong, Polly?"

"Nothing."

"Is it because I mentioned your family?"

I shake my head, and now I feel even more silly. If there's anything to be upset about now, it's them. But I'm not—I'm worried about Harry not actually wanting to be with me. And that just makes me even more selfish, only thinking about myself.

"Then what is it?" He reaches for my hand.

"I'm just worried that we won't work," I say. "And I desperately want us to." I let out a huge breath too quickly and nearly end up choking. "But my last relationship like this, where the guy was allo, didn't work. It just didn't. And I'm just…scared. Scared this is going to turn into that."

He squeezes my hand—lightly though. Like it's just a reassuring gesture, not an overpowering one. "We'll manage it," he says.

"But you're going to think I'm all selfish, not giving you any sex and—"

"Hey." His voice is firm. "I won't. I don't. Polly, it's okay. I mean it. Really, sex isn't that important to me."

"It isn't?" I squint, then stare at the screen of the laptop. The shark is frozen on it. He looks like he's smiling. "But at school, everyone said you slept with everyone."

"Well, not *everyone*. But it was just a coping mechanism really, with my dad's death. I was just looking for the distraction. And I got all that out of my system. Uni helped a lot with that, but after… after I just wanted to be in love—and this is going to sound soppy. But I thought of you, Polly. I wondered about you a lot. And I wanted to see you. When I thought about my future and who I wanted to be with, she always had your face. Always."

"Really?" I stare at him. He felt it too, the connection back at school?

He nods. "And that's why I really want this to work. Polly, I haven't met anyone like you before. And being here with you, it's made me realize it's truly you I want to be with. And it doesn't matter to me that you're ace—like, you're *you*." He leans in closer and kisses my forehead.

I try to relax, but my head's spinning.

"Can I just check one thing though?" he asks, pulling back. "About the whole sex-repulsion thing?"

Immediately, my guard goes straight back up. This is where he reveals that he doesn't actually get it, or didn't realize that I truly meant *no* sex. And so this is where it ends.

I nod, feel my heart slamming against my ribs. I grip the edge of the bed so tight my knuckles go white.

"Okay," Harry says. "So, I get that sex is off the cards—and that's fine," he adds quickly. "Love is more important than sex." His eyes widen, as if he's just realized what he's said. Love is more important than sex. But he doesn't say he loves *me*. He just swallows hastily and continues. "Is that all types of sex? Like, oral too?"

I try to take a deep breath, and I think about changing my answer, trying to make myself sound more appealing in his eyes—only I know what that does to me.

"Yes, it includes that." My voice is a squeak. "I've tried giving before, but..." But I couldn't even bring myself to do it. I just felt pure revulsion at the idea. And it had angered Peter.

"That's perfectly fine," Harry says. "I just need to know where I stand, that's all."

I feel jittery, and I look down, stare at my white knuckles. My fingers feel icy. "Some people have open relationships, when it's like this, but I don't think I can do that—so if it's not going to work, if we're not going to be compatible because of my sexuality, it's best to know now."

"Hey." He touches my face. "It's okay. Look." He tilts my face up, so my eyes meet his. And his are so soft and warm and full of...love? "Polly, we can do this. I know we can. Okay? Love is about compromise."

Love. There it is again. That word. And compromise.

My shoulders sink a bit. Compromise. So why do I feel that Harry's the only one compromising by giving up sex if this relationship goes ahead? I don't feel like I'm making any moves to meet him halfway (something that Peter pointed out once—which made me feel so selfish). I squirm. "I—I can try giving if…" My voice wavers.

He shakes his head. "Polly, you don't need to do that. I don't want you to do something you're not comfortable with or enjoying. You don't need to do anything just to please me." His thumb trails a path down my face, to my jaw. His touch is so tender. "I didn't bring this up to try and get you to agree to stuff, okay? I just wanted to know what is acceptable. You said kissing and cuddling, but like say if we're in bed sometime, how much of your body can I touch?"

I squirm. That's a difficult question to answer. And now even more nervous energy is ricocheting around my body. "Even with physical intimacy that I would be comfortable with at some point, we're going to have to move slowly, okay? Like, build up to it. I can't really answer that question right now. Like, at the moment, kissing—like what we've been doing—and hugging, like that, is okay. But it's going to take me some time to feel comfortable to even think about, I don't know, being naked around you. I'm sorry."

"You don't need to be sorry," he says. "Never apologize for your sexuality or for wanting to go slowly with this. Just guide me okay? You take the lead. And if you're never comfortable with anything, we don't do it. I mean it."

I smile.

"I love you," he says, pulling me in for a hug.

And my eyes are wide against his jacket, and my breathing's fast—and he loves me.

Harry Weller *loves* me.

"I love you too," I whisper into his chest.

TWENTY-SEVEN

Polly

"I THINK WE will be okay," I tell Brooke the next morning. "Me and Harry. We talked a lot last night."

And I feel better now. More comfortable with him. We watched the rest of *Jaws*, and I felt more relaxed after our conversation.

And he said he loves me. But I can't bring myself to tell Brooke that. At the moment, it's my secret. Something just for me that I can hold close to my heart. And I want it just for myself, for a little while longer.

I can't help but smile.

Brooke makes a sound deep in the back of her throat that suggests she has reservations. "I just don't want you getting hurt."

"I know, but like I said, we talked."

"But you and Peter talked too, early on, and you still felt like you had to sleep with him. He made you feel like that."

"But I didn't know I was sex-repulsed then," I say.

"You did," Brooke said. "You told me."

I frown. She's right. I knew deep down, I'd just pretended to myself afterward that I hadn't. It sort of made it easier—

thinking that I had to learn that I was sex-repulsed and the only way to do that was through doing it.

"Harry's not the same as Peter," I finally say.

Brooke nods. "He better not be." She gathers her things. "You coming to breakfast?"

The day seems to drag on and on before I can see Harry, spend time with him properly. There's just so much work to do, but then at last it's the two of us. Alone. Outside.

It's dark. The night air is cool, and the sky is clear. The stars look beautiful.

I take Harry's hand and we walk around the nature reserve. It's amazing how much more comfortable I feel again now. Like, all those worries have just gone. Been lifted away.

Fran was right: communication is important. The most important thing really—and for any relationship. You can't have trust without communication, nor can you truly feel comfortable.

And we're in love, me and Harry. And I can feel it now. The possibility, the hope, that what Fran has with Ivan, I will have with Harry.

As we walk, we talk about random things. A shadow of a tree that looks weird and the call of an owl. Harry wonders what the owl is saying.

"Probably calling for a mate," I say with a shrug.

"Maybe he's searching for his Polly."

I can't help but laugh at that. It sounds so cheesy and ridiculous, but Harry's voice is anything but.

"Maybe it's been eight years since he's seen his Polly, and they've arranged to meet and he can't believe his luck."

I laugh even louder. "Do you believe in Fate?"

He stops and looks at me. His eyes are halos of warmth, and he reaches up, cups my face in his hands. "I didn't. I thought I'd lost you. But something guided me back to you."

"*Word Zero* did."

He snorts. "If my boss ever hears of this, she's going to want a reward or something.

We sit down, and it's amazing how well our bodies fit together. I rest my head against his chest as he holds me close. There's the soft hum of insects not far away, but they're not bothering us. Not like the incessant whining of gnats. No, this feels perfect. Breathing in the cool night air, watching the stars high above, being with Harry.

He traces patterns on my upper arms, and I like the sensation. It grounds me as I look at the stars—so, so far away.

Though Harry's body's radiating heat, it's getting cold out here rapidly, and my legs are numbing.

"We should bring blankets out tomorrow and do this," Harry says. "Just stare up at the stars."

TWENTY-EIGHT

Harry

I GIVE POLLY my coat to wear back, so by the time we reach the accommodation block, I'm colder than I care to admit. But she looks cute with the hood all pulled up around her face. Her nose and cheeks are pink with the temperature, but it makes her eyes look the most amazing green color.

"I'll see you tomorrow then," I say, pulling her close. Her nose is cold, brushing against my face—even with my coat, I think she's colder than me. My arms wrap around her as I kiss her deeply. It is a kiss I've given no one before. One just for her.

And I can't believe this is actually happening. Me and Polly. Not after all those times when we were studying together, and I was dreaming about kissing her, but never did anything— because I didn't want her to end up another one-night-stand like all the other girls I was kissing.

And I thought I'd blown my chance, but wow, Fate must've had greater plans for us.

Us. I like thinking that. Me and Polly. Us.

"I'm on another early shift," Polly says. "Milking." She pulls a face—and it only makes her look even more adorable.

"I'll catch you at lunch then," I say.

We kiss some more—until Brooke opens Polly's door and asks if she's actually going to come in. Polly, face flushed, laughs and pecks me on the cheek before disappearing behind the door.

I can't stop smiling as I head back downstairs to my room. Inside it, I turn up the radiator, then grab a couple of beers from the fridge in my room. The cans are cold—don't do anything for my already-icy hands—but I get them anyway. I suppose it's a habit, and I haven't drunk at all much when I've been at Goldwater. Only the couple times in the games room.

I lounge on my bed, a can in hand, as I scroll through social media. I find myself navigating to Polly's profile, and then I'm scrolling back, eagerly soaking up all the posts she's put up and photos she's been tagged in, as if I can absorb everything about her that I missed in the last eight years.

I must fall asleep looking at photos of Polly—my *girlfriend*—because the next thing I know is someone's pounding at the door.

My heart thumps. Polly?

I open the door and find Lisa. Her face is grave.

"You've got a phone call at the office."

"The office?" I stare at her.

"It's your brother."

Bo. Bo is calling me? It's Mum, it has to be Mum, oh God.

Everything spins around me as I follow Lisa to the office. I can hardly think straight and my heart's pounding too much. I feel sicker and sicker with every step, and then we're at the office and Lisa's giving me the phone, and then she's leaving.

The air feels too thick. I lift the receiver to my ear.

"Hello?"

"Harry," Bo says. "You need to get a flight up here right now. Mum's had a heart attack."

A heart attack?

I take a step back, stumble against the desk. Something clatters to the floor. My breathing is a rushing sound in my ears, and Bo's still talking, but I can't make out what he's saying. All I can hear are the words *heart attack*, over and over in my head, echoing louder and louder with each time.

I slump to the ground, cradling the phone. "Is she going to be okay?"

"You need to get here now, Harry."

Morris's room is next to the office and I nearly knock down his door, the way I'm pummeling it with my fists.

He answers it, blinking sleepily.

"I've got to get out of here," I shout. "Can you drive me?"

Morris gives me a look. "We're in lockdown, mate." His Australian accent seems even stronger. "You can't leave."

Panic surges within me. "You don't understand... it's an emergency." My heart thrums. A car... I need a car... But I've had beers. I might be over the limit...and in any case, I can't drive in this state. I can never drive when I'm wound up. "I've got to get out..." I run a hand through my hair.

But Morris is shaking his head as he shuts the door. And then the door's shut, and....

Oh my God.

"No," I mutter.

I turn.

There's a figure standing in the stairwell. Evie.

She approaches me. "I'll drive you. I think I need to get to a walk-in center too. Pain's getting worse," she says, but I can't focus on anything she's saying. All I can focus on is my mum.

"She's had a heart attack," I say. "My Mum."

Evie's eyes widen. "Oh, Harry," she says, and then she's hugging me. "It'll be okay. Come on, we'll go now."

TWENTY-NINE

Polly

THE NEXT MORNING dawns bright and early, and I've got a definite spring in my step (as much as that is a cliché) as I set about doing the daily work. Even if it involves milking the Friesians—meaning I miss Harry at breakfast, because of having to get up so early, and spend my morning working with animals I'm not especially fond of. Not to mention I don't like the hum of the electricity in the milking sheds. It always makes me uneasy.

But I smile as I think of seeing Harry at lunch, and then again tonight, with how we planned to get some blankets and lie under the stars, like we did last night. Only five short hours ago. I yawn.

George is also on milking today, along with Morris who keeps grumbling about being awoken at an 'ungodly hour.' Best to steer well clear of him. Morris on no sleep is not a good thing to encounter.

Still, the work keeps me busy until lunch time.

I shower quickly, change into fresh clothes and consider putting on makeup for the first time in a long time. Just a little bit—mainly because I'm terrible at putting it on. I settle for some mascara. That's it. And I have to borrow that from Brooke's drawer anyway.

I hum under my breath as I make my way to the canteen.

"...going to be in so much trouble," Grant is saying as I get there.

"No excuse," Jane replies.

"What's going on?" I slide into a chair next to Brooke, then look around for Harry. I can't see him. Maybe he's still absorbed in his work.

Brooke looks at me with wide eyes—the kind of eyes that I know immediately. The hairs on the back of my neck rise.

"What is it?"

She shakes her head. "I'm sorry, Polly. But he's gone." Her face is like thunder, and she rubs her bare shoulder where her eagle tattoo is. "Harry's left."

"Left?" I frown, then start to laugh. Then I stop when no one else is laughing.

"Grant saw him and Evie hugging and then driving off. They've both broken lockdown to run away. I'm so sorry."

THIRTY

Polly

THERE HAS TO be some sort of mistake. There has to be. That's all I can think. Harry and I…we're strong. He wouldn't just run off with Evie.

How can you think you're strong? You've only been together a couple days.

I feel sick as I stare at Brooke, then realize everyone's staring at me.

Harry broke lockdown to leave. And with Evie.

Everything inside me crumples, and I run from the room.

"Polly!" Brooke shouts after me.

I turn and shake my head. "I need to be on my own."

Up in my room, I feel…empty. I feel nothing. Well, there's the nausea and sadness, and…disbelief that he's done this. Then there's the indignation, the refusal to accept it. I must be wrong. Harry wouldn't do that.

But he has.

I try phoning him, angrily hitting the screen of my phone as I select his contact. It rings and rings. He doesn't answer.

Steeling myself, I try Evie. She doesn't answer either.

I squeeze my eyes shut just as hot tears attempt to leak out of the corners of them. How could I have been so stupid to think this would work? That he'd seriously be interested in me? And he wouldn't even tell me face-to-face. Or even a text.

He just left. Left with Evie.

Left without telling me, without leaving me *anything*.

I feel sicker than ever.

Half an hour later, Brooke lets herself into the room.

"Don't," I say to her. I don't want to hear how she was right. Oh, God. Why didn't I just listen to her?

"I'm not," she says. "But shift's have started again. I've swapped with Grant, so you're with me. Come on."

She puts my laptop in her bag and leads me away, and I feel like I'm not even here as I follow her first to the research center where she grabs a binder, and then to the viewing hut. She hands me the records that need digitizing, and I start on the work, not even questioning what we're doing given all research jobs had been put on hold before. I just like having the distraction. My fingertips burn as I type, and I gulp several times.

Brooke's hunched over a stool at the other desk, working diligently, her head bent close so her eyes are inches away from what she's writing. The radio in the back of her belt flashes an amber light every thirty seconds. It's low on battery. Needs charging.

I type more numbers into my spreadsheet.

How could Harry do this?

I pull my phone out, check it for any calls or messages from him. Nothing.

Nothing at all.

Tears blind me, and I want to scream. But I don't.

I wipe my eyes and I keep entering numbers onto the laptop, stabbing each key so hard a little pain reverberates through my arm.

"Easy," Brooke says at one point.

And I must be losing time, because then we're heading back to the canteen for dinner. And I don't want to go in there where everyone will stare at me and know that Harry's left me for Evie, but it's like I'm not in control of my body. I just follow Brooke, like I'm on autopilot.

Everyone else is already in the canteen, and they're crowded around the TV. Brooke and I edge closer.

"Yes, I can confirm that as of thirty minutes ago, the remaining two men have been caught," the reporter says. She's smiling. It's always her, the same reporter, and this is the happiest she's looked in days.

There are cheers all around and shouts of being free at last.

I'm the only one who doesn't cheer. I just move through my haze to the hot food hatch. I ladle some soup into a bowl, grab a bread roll and then sit at the nearest table. It's not even the table I normally sit at with Brooke.

But no one notices.

Everyone is too busy celebrating.

My phone pings. My heart soars and I pull it from my pocket. Harry?

It's not.

Just an email. I click on it. From the dating holiday company. At last, they've replied to my email.

Hi Miss Brady,

Not to worry. You're more than welcome to join us when you can. I've just seen the lockdown's been lifted. I'll reimburse you for the days you couldn't attend.

All best,

Mrs. Mitchell

I stare at the email. The dating holiday, where I was supposed to be all along. Maybe…maybe I should go. I need to get out of here. And it is my holiday time right now. Now lockdown's over and other staff can get in, I can't be expected to work.

Brooke's heading toward me, so I hold up my phone, show it to her. Her expression darkens immediately—maybe thinking it's from Harry—but then she reads it and sits down.

"You going to go?" she asks.

I shrug, stirring my soup. It's tomato. I don't even like tomato. "Maybe."

"I think that's best," she says. "You can't let Harry get to you like this."

THIRTY-ONE

Harry

"SHE'S JUST ALONG here," Bo tells me.

I'm hot and sweaty and barely functioning as I follow him through the hospital corridors. The last few hours have been a blur. Evie drove me straight to the nearest airport, only to find that the flights to Edinburgh had been cancelled. She then drove me farther north and I got a plane there. A few hours later, I was meeting with Bo—and my brother's never looked so worried.

The room he leads me to is small but bright and airy. I see Sara in there already, leaning over a frail figure in the bed. Mum. The roof of my mouth dries.

Mum looks weaker and smaller than I remembered. Bonier, like she's not been eating. It's been a few years since I've seen her, and I immediately feel guilty for that.

Her eyes light up though as she sees me. "Harrison," she croaks, because of course even now she won't use the shortened version of my name. She reaches out for me with one thin arm, and Sara moves out of the way so I can hug Mum.

She doesn't smell the same though. She smells of hospital.

Loads of wires spider from her chest, and there are machines clicking and beeping.

After hugging Mum, I turn to Sara and Bo. "What have the doctors said?"

"That she's lucky," Sara says. She doesn't look at me, but at least she's talking to me. That's something. "They didn't think she'd survive the operation; her blood pressure was all out of whack."

I rub the back of my neck. My fingers feel greasy with travel, and now it's all over my neck too. I let out a sigh, and then Sara's explaining more in very medical terms that I don't understand. But my sister's a carer, she gets these sorts of things. I don't.

I pat my pocket for my phone, but of course it's not there. I curse again—just as I cursed when I got to the airport and realized it was still in my room at Goldwater. I'd been about to text Polly then to let her know what's happening.

I wince. I still need to let Polly know where I am. She's going to be worried—and disappearing in the middle of lockdown. Even if…didn't someone on the plane say it had been lifted? I don't know. I'm sleep-deprived. Can't think sense. Think I imagined it.

"My children, all back together again," Mum suddenly says.

The three of us turn to look at her. She's smiling a toothless smile.

I stay in Glasgow, at Bo's, for a day. Sara's here too, and I don't think my brother can take having his siblings at his house for a moment longer. But the doctors have reassured us Mum will be fine, and Sara's going to have her moved in with her, in Newcastle. It's too dangerous for Mum to live alone now.

I promise to visit more frequently—and I mean it. But I'm also desperate to get out of this house. I need to phone Polly—she must be out of her mind. But I haven't got her number on me, and there's no internet at Bo's. He said a storm took it out two days ago and he's still waiting on engineers to come and repair it.

When at last I can leave, I feel almost bad. Like I'm turning my back on my family—but I will be back. And I'll bring Polly. I told Sara and Bo about me and Polly last night. Bo nodded, and Sara looked disinterested—but I suppose she would. She doesn't like me because I slept with her best friend and then never called her the next morning. It was years ago though. How was I to know that Sara's best friend was in love with me?

Bo drops me off at the airport, and it's a relatively quick flight with no delays back down to Devon, especially when all Devon airports are open now. On the newspapers at the airports, I see mugshots of the four men—all of whom have now been located and are being held somewhere secure.

By the time I get to Goldwater, it's dark. I've been away two days, and suddenly it feels much longer. There's no one to let me in at the gates, and the gates are bolted right across. I press the buzzer and wait. My legs are whirring with the walk—the nearest bus from the airport dropped me off six miles from here.

The intercom makes a clicking sound. "Hello? Can I help you?"

"Brooke?" I step closer. "It's me, Harry. I'm back and—"

"What the hell are you doing?" She does not sound happy.

"Can you just let me in?"

"No," she says. "I'm coming down."

It takes Brooke exactly four and a half minutes to get to the gate. She doesn't look happy to see me. Her eyes are full of anger, and there's only hardness to her expression. She's wearing her oversized fur coat and that just makes her look more formidable, especially in the dark.

I step forward as she reaches the gate. She doesn't unlock it, just looks at me through the bars. "Please, can you let me in?"

She shakes her head.

"Brooke, all my stuff is in there!"

"So it's just your stuff you care about?" She raises her eyebrows.

"What?"

"Not Polly then?" She snorts. "Should've known what you're like."

"Polly—of course I want to see Polly."

"Oh, you do? That's convenient. Where is she anyway?" She's looking behind me. "Evie?"

"Evie?" I frown. "I don't know. I thought she came back here after she drove me?"

Brooke presses her lips together so tightly they seem to disappear. "I'll bring your stuff to the gates," she says. "But you're not coming in."

"Why?" I stare at her, frowning. "What's going on?"

"You're really playing the whole innocent card, Harry? Seriously? You leave Polly for Evie and think you can play at being innocent about this whole thing? Huh, well, I don't think so. Not when you left her for Evie."

"What?" I squint, stare at her. "I didn't."

"You drove off with Evie in *the middle of the night.*" Her eyes flash. "When we were in lockdown, no less. When no one was allowed to move, and the two of you still left. And you didn't even tell Polly."

Nearby, I hear an engine start up. One of the patrol trucks. I'd recognize it anywhere.

"She had to learn it from us. Do you know how broken she looked when she found out? That you'd chosen Evie over her?"

"That's not what happened!" I shout. "Evie just drove me to the airport. I had to get to Edinburgh. My mum had a heart attack."

Brooke's eyes widen. "What?" Her voice is small.

"I had to get there—she's fine, as it happens. But Evie was the only one who'd drive me out, under lockdown. Oh! She said she was going to a walk-in center or something." I'd forgotten that.

"For her bladder?" Now, Brooke sounds worried.

"What?"

"Harry, she's got Interstitial Cystitis. Often has to go to get catherization or something done. She usually tells us when she's going there and… " She waves the rest of her sentence away with her hand. "Why didn't you phone Polly? Or text or anything?"

"I haven't got my phone with me. It's in my room. At Goldwater," I add. "Now, can you please let me in. I need to see Polly, set her straight about this."

"You... You're too late," Brooke whispers. "That was Morris taking Polly to the airport."

"The airport?" I stare at her.

"They're going out the north gate."

"But why's she going to the airport?" Everything in my chest tightens.

"She was supposed to go on a dating holiday for other asexuals—you know, people who wouldn't break her heart—right before this lockdown. Now it's lifted, and you'd disappeared, we encouraged her to go."

The ground beneath me suddenly seems too soft, too insubstantial. Polly thinks I don't love her. She's going on dating holiday.

"Which airport?" I bark to Brooke. "I've got to get there."

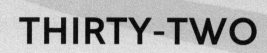

THIRTY-TWO

Polly

"YES, THE FLIGHT'S just about to board now," the flight attendant tells me. He looks tired, but he's still trying to smile brightly. At least he can still put up a pretense. I, on the other hand, look a mess. I caught a glimpse of myself in one of the windows of the airport shops earlier—my hair's a mess, my face is clearly tear-stained, and I look frazzled.

"Polly!"

The shout's loud and...

Harry?

It can't be.

I strain my eyes, trying to see him through the crowd.

It is him.

"Harry?"

He's running toward me, and a security guard is trying to stop him. And everyone's looking.

"What are you doing?" I shout at him. "You and Evie..." My heart pounds, and I look around for her. Is she here too?

"There's nothing going on between me and Evie," he says, panting as he reaches me. "She just drove me to the airport.

Mum had a heart attack. I had to go and I left so quickly, there was barely any time. And I forgot my phone and—"

"Is your mum okay?" My eyes are wide.

Harry nods.

"Sir, if you don't come with us we will have to forcibly remove you," the security man says.

"Polly, please don't get on that plane," Harry shouts. His voice is frantic now. "It's just a misunderstanding. I love you."

"It's okay," I say, "I won't."

And then Harry's being pulled back by the security man and he's shouting, and I'm shouting.

"It's okay, we're both leaving," I say. "Sorry for the mix up."

"Ma'am, your plane is boarding," the flight attendant says.

"It's okay," I say, "I'm not getting on it." I look around. "My luggage. Where's my luggage?"

"All bags have already gone through," the flight attendant says.

"I need my bag!"

"We're really sorry about this," Harry says. "But can you get her bag back?"

The security guard is giving us evil looks and the flight attendant looks even more worn out.

"I'll see what I can do," the flight attendant finally says.

I breathe a sigh of relief, and then Harry sweeps me into an embrace.

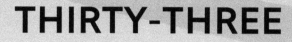

THIRTY-THREE

Polly

Two Years Later

"CONGRATULATIONS!" BROOKE CANNOT stop smiling. She's grinning from ear to ear, and I've never seen her look so happy. Or so unlike-Brooke. She's got flowers in her hair and a pale mauve dress on, just like the other bridesmaids.

She sweeps me into a hug and I'm just careful enough not to trip over my dress. Over Brooke's shoulder I see Fran and Ivan and they're both smiling warmly.

And this—this is the happiest day of my life.

He's standing just to the right of Fran, posing for a photo with Morris and Grant. Freddie, Brooke and Grant's one-year-old son, is in Grant's arms and he's reaching out for the bow tie that Grant's got on. It's the same bow tie all the men have got on here. The crocodile bow ties.

When Brooke and I found the box of them before the wedding, she said every man attending had to wear them. And all the men are.

My grin gets wider.

Freddie sees me and reaches out for me, even from Grant's arms, like he believes he can reach me just by stretching his chubby little arm out. And Freddie is cute. Since he was born, Harry and I have talked more about whether we'll have kids. I mean, shortly after he met me at the airport, we had the whole conversation about kids. Harry wants them, and I think I do. And Harry suggested adoption.

"Mind if I have a dance with her?" my husband says as he approaches me and Brooke.

Brooke steps away, smiling as she goes for her son. She kisses Grant on the cheek as she lifts Freddie away from him, then she's soaring her son through the air, all the while making squawking noises that have Freddie giggling.

I turn to my husband.

"A dance? Out here?"

The reception's being held at Goldwater—where else would it be held?—but the sky's threatening rain.

"Of course," my husband says.

He takes my hands and leads me forward. People start cheering. To the right is Lisa. She's been amazing with the organizing of this—even if she did want the guests to play musical chairs. Shu-li and James, Brooke's parents, along with her grandmother Hsiao-han, are here. Right before the ceremony, Hsiao-han cornered me, tears in her eyes as she smiled and hugged me before giving me a red gown. "For later," she said, and she explained it had been her dress and how at her wedding, many years ago, she changed outfit many times. "Red is good luck."

And the luck has worked, I know that now. Because today has been perfect. And I don't know why, but I'd convinced myself something would go wrong. But it hasn't. It's as perfect as it can be.

Evie is here too, and she's smiling, standing with Jane and George. She's not one of my bridesmaids—only Brooke and Fran are—and I felt a bit weird inviting her, since she left Goldwater pretty soon after she took Harry to the airport. I think part of her decision to leave was because she still liked Harry and he'd managed to get a job at Goldwater, so she didn't want to see him every day. But I spoke to her earlier, and she was telling me about her new job—something in admin—and she seemed happy. And I am glad she is here.

She did, after all, help my husband.

And I look up into my husband's face and smile.

Harry Weller is mine.

Note from the Author:
Resources on Asexuality

Hi there! If you are on the asexual spectrum, or are questioning whether you are, there are a lot of resources and support groups out there to help you understand asexuality and make you feel less alone. And feeling less alone and knowing that there are other people like me out there was a huge thing for me when I was realizing I was ace.

I found the following resources invaluable, particularly in the years where I was just coming to grips with what my sexuality meant for me, so I hope that this list can be of some help to others too.

The Asexual Visibility and Education Network (AVEN): www.asexuality.org

AVEN forums: www.asexuality.org

Asexualitic, a place to meet other asexuals: www.asexualitic.com/forums/

The Trevor Project, supporting LGBT youth:
www.thetrevorproject.org/trvr_support_center/
asexual/

Find local Meetups with those who identify as part of the asexuality spectrum:
www.meetup.com/topics/asexuality/

"Feeling isolated as an asexual in a sexualised society":
www.bbc.co.uk/news/magazine-41569900

Asexual Aces Facebook Page:
www.facebook.com/a.aces.page/

A Safe Ace Place, Facebook Support Group for Asexuals:
www.facebook.com/groups/1528186337398691/

Acknowledgments

In My Dreams has been so much fun to write, but it's also been a really important story for me to tell. It came about following a conversation I had with Crystal Lacy (an amazing m/m romance writer!) where we talked about how my own sexuality (asexuality) isn't often seen in romance books. Crystal was extremely encouraging of me writing an own-voices ace romance—and so this is just such a book! I'm honestly not sure I would've ever decided to write this book without Crystal's support and encouragement—so thank you, Crystal!

And wow, I can't believe how validating writing this book has been. Delving into Polly and Harry's romance was refreshing and so much fun. And it's made me realize that ace romance is something I need to write more of. Long ago, I dreamed of being a romance writer, but I always assumed I'd have to write books with sex in, thinking then that romance readers wouldn't want a book where there was no sex at all between the main couple, not even any that was implied! But because of Crystal's encouragement I wrote this book—and I found that ace romance is what *really* calls to me. These are the stories I need to tell. And just talking with others in the Ace Community has really cemented my desire to write more of these. We need diversity in romance!

A huge thank you must go to my editor, Isvari Mohan Maranwe, for your insightful comments and edits that helped me fine-tune this story. To Sarah Anderson: you're an amazing critique partner, and your enthusiasm for this story really kept me going—even on those days when I was sure no one would want to read this. And to my writer friends—Lisa Amowitz, Emily Colin, Heidi Ayarbe, Megan Eccles, and Janelle Alexander—thank you for all your unwavering support.

Heather Walker, thank you so much for your amazing narration for the audiobook. The first time I heard you bringing to life Polly and Harry's story, I was blown away.

To my mum and dad—thank you for being supportive of me when I came out to you about my sexuality, and for (of course) supporting my writing. Your support means a lot to me.

And, finally, to my readers: thank you for picking up this book. I hope you've enjoyed it.

About the Author

ELIN ANNALISE writes contemporary romances with ace characters. She graduated from Exeter University in 2016, where she studied English literature and watched the baby rabbits play on the lawns when she should've been taking notes on Milton and Homer. She's a big fan of koi carp, cats, and dreaming.

She's the author of *In My Dreams, My Heart to Find,* and *It's Always Been You.*

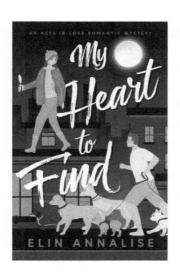

AN ACES IN LOVE ROMANTIC MYSTERY

MY HEART TO FIND

Avid crime-fiction-reader Cara Tate is twenty-five years old, shy, asexual, and desperate to find love. But there's a problem: Cara's chronic Lyme disease has caused brain inflammation and OCD that makes her afraid of anyone touching her. Plus, finding other aces isn't easy—especially when there's no guarantee of a connection.

But there is one man Cara knows who is ace and whom she feels something for. One man who she might just be able to hug...or more. If she can summon the courage to defy the control of her OCD.

Three years ago, when Cara was healthy, she and her ace best friend Jana went on a retreat for those on the asexual spectrum. There, she met professional dog-walker and true-crime-fanatic Damien Noelle—the only man she's ever felt a connection with. But she was too nervous to stay in contact with Damien after the retreat and has spent the last three years strongly regretting it.

So when Fate has her path cross with Damien once more, and they have the chance to investigate a real-life crime together, Cara's determined to overcome her shyness and OCD and let him know she's more than interested. The only problem is Damien seems interested in Jana now, and the last thing Cara wants to do is ruin her friend's happiness. For the last few months, Jana's been dealing with the boss from hell, and Cara knows Damien could be the best thing Jana's had all year. She can't take that away from her best friend... can she?

My Heart to Find is *an #ownvoices story for asexuality and chronic illness representation (Lyme Disease and Encephalitis-induced OCD, also known as PANS).*

My Heart to Find

SNEAK PEAK

ONE

Cara

IF THERE'S ONE place I never want to be again, it's in this club with the too-loud music and the too-hot artificial glares.

My head pounds, and my vision blurs. A grating sensation—the usual one—fills my head. It feels like a miniscule drill is digging into my skull. I wince as the pain comes. Three flashes of it. The pain is like a volcano, hot and bubbling and consuming, leaving me panting and breathless. Dark spots hover in front of my eyes for a moment. My chest shudders, but it shudders out of sync with the rest of my body, creating a jarring sensation.

I grunt. Well they can't say I'm *boring* now. And I try to focus on that—my triumph at proving River and everyone else who wrote mean stuff about me online wrong. Because *boring people* don't go to clubs. *Boring people* don't try to dance under bright lights—even if I didn't quite manage it because I couldn't go too near other people. But *boring people* are tucked up in bed at this ungodly hour, not dancing the night away.

Not that I'm dancing. My body's too broken for that.

Not that I'm boring either—I'm chronically ill. There's a world of difference. I shouldn't have let the nasty comments get to me. Jana told me not to. She said I've got nothing to prove by coming out here.

But she doesn't get it. She doesn't live a life where she's referred to as *the sick girl* or *the psycho* or *the boring, ill one* or the *faker*. And maybe forcing myself to come out to this club with Jana was a bad idea because it could fuel the 'faker' rumors, making it seem that I'm actually well enough to be here.

And I'm not.

I'm *so* not.

"Do you want to go outside?"

I look up. A man's staring at me from a few feet away—concerned? I mean, no wonder; I have sweat pouring off me. His face is also shiny with perspiration, albeit not as much as I can feel on mine . The flashing lights make his skin look an eerie green, but they also emphasize the strong, heavy features of his face. A slightly hooked nose. Thick eyebrows. He'd be great to draw a caricature of. Could easily be a villain in my cartoon strip.

I breathe deeply. Yes. I need fresh air.

I need to get out of here.

"Definitely," I shout back, but I can't even hear my own voice over the pounding music.

I look around. I lost sight of Jana at least half an hour ago. Well, she's probably outside too. Clubs aren't really her scene. We're only here because it's her cousin's birthday. And Anastacia is one of those people that you don't say no to.

The man reaches for my hand—

No!

I flinch as he makes contact. I pull my hand back quickly, and my breathing quickens. He gives me an odd look, then gestures for me to walk ahead of him in the direction of an exit.

I do, the whole time trying to still my racing mind. My fingers feel burnt where he touched them. I want to wipe them on something. Hell, even wash them. But the bathroom here is full of vomiting teenagers, and I can't go in there, no matter how strong the urge to wash my hands—or to empty my bladder—gets. And I can't wipe my hands on my dress. I just can't. Getting outside—into the fresh air—sounds good, even though most of the time I'm scared of the outdoors, of all the dangers it holds. But being outdoors is now preferable to being stuck in here, with sweat particles in the air, and the heavy breaths of clubbers sticking to me....

It's okay, I tell myself. *It's okay.*

I'll shower when I get home, of course I will. No matter how sick I'm feeling, no matter how much my head is pounding and my stomach's churning. No matter how much my swollen, aching knees and lower back are begging me to just sit down for a moment, I won't because I will shower first.

But you won't be able to get your phone from your bag without washing your hands first.

I ignore that thought. The OCD. It's controlling, as always. Even out here. Even when I know I'm going to shower and thoroughly decontaminate myself.

I squeeze through dancing bodies, wincing with every accidental contact I make, and then I'm outside.

We're outside. The man grins at me, leans against the wall, tells me his name is Rob.

Well, I think his name is Rob. My ears are still ringing and there's a low roaring filling my head. Could've been Bob. Bob— nah, that sounds too old for a man this young. I take a deep breath. We're the only ones out here. Jana's not here. My gaze goes back to the door of the club. She must still be in there.

"So," Rob says. "Nice evening."

"Y-y-y…yes," I say, cringing at my usual speech problems. The sounds just get stuck in my mouth. Or sometimes they don't even get to my mouth; I often can't seem to translate what I'm thinking into words. But, at least here, I'll just sound like I'm drunk. This man won't know I've got a severe chronic illness. He's just Rob. Rob the… I try to work out what his character would be in my cartoon. Rob the Robber? Nah, that's silly. Rob the… But I don't know what he's like, whether he's a good guy or not, and that's important in my characters' names.

Unless I do run with that name. Rob the Robber. Make him a bad guy.

My eyes fall on a puddle of vomit near his feet. Revulsion pulls through me, and my skin starts to crawl. The OCD tries to tell me that the vomit's on me, that somehow particles of it are in the air and now are clinging to me. I try to ignore the voice as best as I can.

Rob the Robber must see me staring at the vomit, because he grunts and steps away. "It's those kids nowadays, they don't know how to hold their drink."

I look back at his face. Out here, in the near dark with one flickering streetlight, he looks more human, but older too. Late thirties? My stomach does a little flutter at that.

I hold onto my bag tighter—the little clutch bag I only ever use for this sort of stuff. Parties. Clubs. The things that aren't me at all. Inside my clutch bag is a jiffy bag with my phone, keys, ID, meds, and debit card in it. Couldn't put them straight in my bag. The OCD told me that'd be too dangerous.

Rob steps closer.

"What are you doing?" Alarm fills my voice.

He gives me a strange look. "Uh, how are we going to hookup if we stay ten feet apart?"

I step back. The back of my arm catches the rough brick wall, and I flinch. My sudden movement sends a serpent of pain down my left leg. "I'm not having sex with you." Or doing anything with him! Is...is that what he thinks is going to happen?

He looks around. "Yeah, s'pose it's not the nicest. We can go back to mine. Come on."

"Uh... no." I swallow hard. My eyes feel strange. This can't be happening. It *can't* be.

Rob's eyes narrow. "You've been leading me on?"

Leading him on? What the hell? I hadn't even danced with him—or even met him five minutes ago.

But you did agree to come out here with him.

I look back to the club. I need to get back inside there. Need to find Jana and Anastacia and her friends. Not be out here alone with this man. And it's not like we're at the front of the club, on the road with easy getaway access. We're at the back. A secluded vomit-splattered patio. "I don't go back to people's houses," I say.

"*People's* houses." He snorts. His tone becomes slightly menacing. "I'm not people."

"I don't do this sort of stuff though." My fingers are ice-cold. I take a step toward the door.

"Ah, you can have a bit of fun," he says. "Come on, we're both attracted to each other. You wouldn't have come out here with me otherwise."

I am not attracted to him—not at all, and especially not sexually. But there's no way I'm telling him that—or that I'm ace. He could flip out on me; it's happened before. I've got to put my safety first.

This was a bad idea. How stupid was I to think all going to a club was a good idea? Not just with my OCD but with being on the asexual spectrum too?

"Clubs aren't just for finding hookups," Jana had said earlier when I'd expressed doubt. "They're for having fun." And she's always saying I need to have more fun. My stomach tightens. I wonder if she agrees with those comments left on my profile—that I'm boring.

And maybe I do need to have more fun, because my life is just one hospital appointment after another, one episode of OCD after another, one crying session after another.

But looking at Rob now, with that glint in his eye, makes me wonder what exactly I've let myself into by coming out to "have fun."

My throat feels too thick and my mouth too dry, and suddenly I'm thinking about the woman who went missing two weeks ago. Marnie Wathem, a nineteen-year-old disappeared when walking some dogs. She's the talk of the town, and most people are saying she's just a runaway. That's the stance the cops have taken too; it's easier to believe nothing bad happens in Brackerwood, and also gives the police less work. But Marnie's brother has been adamant the whole time that she was abducted—or worse. He tried to get media attention on his views to prompt the police to do something, but that didn't work.

And I think he could be onto something. I mean, I read a lot of crime fiction, and so many of those books start with a similar situation where the town doesn't even realize a crime has taken place until it's too late. So many nights recently, I've thought about Marnie, let my half-dreaming brain conjure up all sorts of scenarios where, somehow, I'm the one who saves her.

But now, with Rob in front of me, I know I wouldn't be brave enough to save Marnie. I'm shaking so much, and I'm freezing up.

"I'm sorry, I can't do this," I say, trying to keep my voice as unconfrontational as possible. Because bad things can happen anywhere. Was Marnie really abducted? And my head is spinning and suddenly I'm convinced that the man in front of me is responsible.

I'm going to be his second victim.

But then Rob nods. "Okay."

He kicks at the gravel to the side of the patio, watches the stones cascade across the concrete slabs beyond, and then heads back to the club.

I breathe out a huge sigh of relief and follow. My heart pounds—did I really just avoid a dangerous situation or was that just my imagination? Hot air blasts back over me, and the music seems even louder than before. Rob's gone, disappeared into a mass of bodies, and I hold my bag close, my fingers shaking as I search for my friend.

"Jana!" I find her by the DJ, where the music's the loudest and most deafening. She looks bored as she stares at a couple who are making out.

With a jolt, I realize that the guy in the embrace is Jana's ex, Max. And the girl is Anastacia, her cousin. Wow. Anastacia the *Awful*.

"You ready to go?" Jana asks me, her eyes brightening. She twists the black ring on her finger.

"I nod. Let's get out of here," I say, looking around again in case Rob's watching. I can't see him. My stomach feels empty and slimy, and it's making me feel sicker now—both because of my illness, my medications, and the situation I narrowly avoided—but I also know I haven't eaten in a while. "We can get takeaway."

I know Jana's always up for chips, especially when she's had a drink or few. And I need to take my night-time meds, I should've already had them by this hour, and they have to be taken with food.

We say goodbye to Anastacia—not that she unlocks herself from Max's lips long enough to speak—and head out.

"I can't believe her," Jana says as we exit the club and step out into the high street. "She just *launched* herself at him…"

I make sympathetic noises—or, at least, I think I do. But I can tell my reactions are slow, and maybe they're so slow they don't leave my mouth at all. Because my mind is still on Rob.

What if he hadn't accepted no for an answer?

No, don't think of that. You're safe. Nothing happened.

"And he didn't exactly put up much of a fight, did he?" Jana huffs. "God, he can't even keep it in his pants. I was stupid to think he was ever okay with me being ace."

"Because that's what he told you," I say, and I have to concentrate on each word. I think I sound very drunk. "But don't think about that now."

She exhales sharply, digging a cigarette and lighter out of her bag. She checks which way the wind's blowing before lighting it—so the smoke won't blow over me, she's always very particular about that—and then swears loudly. About Max.

I do my best to pacify her, but the heaviness is taking over my body again. That and the OCD is picking up. Even though the smoke isn't directly going over me, I imagine it as a dusty blanket settling on my skin and dress and bag and hair.

You'll never get it out, the OCD whispers.

I try to ignore it. Focus on my surroundings—the streetlights, the red taillights of cars, the crisp, night air. On how even *if* there is smoke on me, it won't do me any harm. That's what my therapist says. And the psychiatrist too. And, anyway, I'm showering as soon as I get home. And then I can grab my graphics tablet and work some more on my cartoon strip to calm me before I sleep. I could draw some new caricatures. Maybe Jana. She features regularly in my art. Jana the Jewel, one of the main characters of my story. But she could be Jana the…Jazzy, too?

We pass a streetlight with one of the missing posters for Marnie Wathem tacked onto it. Her pale blue eyes set in her pale face seem to latch onto me as we walk past, and even once we're a block away from that poster, I still feel like the missing woman's watching me. It makes me shudder.

The chip shop is in sight now, and there's a man coming out of it, hands in his pockets, looking all casual and nonchalant. But there's something familiar about him, about the way his blond hair flops over his face. How he walks with confidence, but he also manages to look casual too.

"Is that…?" I stop, squinting ahead.

"What?" Jana asks with a grunt.

It's Damien. I inhale sharply. Damien Noelle. My eyes widen.

He hasn't seen me, and my heart's pounding, and I'm glad he hasn't seen me. So glad. My knees weaken, and I'm nervous—*of course* I'm nervous.

It's *him*.

My palms are sweating, and suddenly, it's like I'm back there, three years ago in Mallorca, on the retreat for those on the asexual spectrum, watching Damien Noelle make eye contact with me across the room. Eye contact that makes me giddy. Because he's *hot*.

Flashes of the rest of the two weeks and the time afterward fill my mind: Damien and me talking; Damien and me lounging in the games room; Damien telling me we'd have to meet up again back in England; Damien writing his number on the inside page of the book I was reading; me being too shy to call at first, and then realizing I'd lost the book when I was finally about to pick up my phone.

I swallow hard. How can he *be* here? I mean, what are the chances? The one guy I've been dreaming of bumping into again, more often than I'd like to admit, is *here*.

A numbness travels down the back of my right thigh.

"Nah, no one," I say, because if I tell Jana it's him, she'll make me go over and see him. Make me *talk* to him. And I can't talk to guys I like. I mean, sure I talked to Damien on the retreat, but that felt different. In Mallorca, I could almost be someone else. Someone confident. But here, I'm not confident. Not with guys. I'm shy and awkward. And I can't have Jana forcing me to go and talk to him, even if she thinks she's helping me.

Or Jana will have completely forgotten who he is. It's been three years, after all. Just because I think about Damien almost every day—regretting that I didn't decide to call him sooner—doesn't mean Jana will even remember him. I mean, most of the time on the retreat she was with Ray, a guy who's graysexual like her.

Unlike my relationship—if you could even call what Damien and I had on the retreat a 'relationship'—Jana's had survived the plane journey back. Ray lived in the midlands and they'd ended up in a long-distance relationship for a year after the retreat until they realized neither was willing to relocate. Jana has to stay in the area as she looks after her sister's kids when her sister's at work. And it was shortly after that breakup that she met Max the Moron, a straight guy who told her he was fine with her being on the ace spectrum.

But he wasn't.

Still, at least she's *had* relationships.

I haven't. Not one. I'm twenty-five and I've never been kissed—even if at several points on that retreat, I'd thought that Damien and I would. But we were both nervous, both cautiously dancing around each other, trying to figure each other out.

My eyes linger on Damien as he walks away. I breathe a sigh of relief. He didn't see me.

MY HEART TO FIND IS AVAILABLE NOW!

WANT EVEN MORE FROM THE ACES IN LOVE SERIES?

IT'S ALWAYS BEEN YOU

Twenty-six-year-old Courtney Davenport is loud, fun, and always the heart of a party. She's also asexual and runs a talking service for other aces who are worried about coming out.

But when her sworn enemy Sophie Sway phones the helpline, Courtney is thrown.

Courtney and Sophie have been enemies forever. Growing up at an expensive boarding school that pitted them against each other has ensured their rivalry lasted way beyond graduation. And now Sophie's not just coming out to her—unknowing that it is Courtney at the end of the line—but worse! In the coincidence of the century, Sophie's also moving next door.

Furious, Courtney decides to do everything in her power to make Sophie think her new apartment is haunted, so she'll move away. But then the two of them are invited to participate in a reality-style TV show where their rivalry is turned into a game. Now, there's no way Courtney can get away from Sophie as each of them is encouraged to carry out more and more elaborate pranks on the other in order to be crowned the winner.

And the more time Courtney spends around Sophie, the more she begins to question her feelings about her...

After all, love is a small step away from hate.

Each book in the Aces in Love *series can be read as a standalone; no prior knowledge of the series is needed to enjoy these stories!*

CPSIA information can be obtained
at www.ICGtesting.com
Printed in the USA
LVHW092227120222
710709LV00008BA/761

9 781912 369287